LIGHT INSPIRED

a novel by
Anuradha Bhattacharyya

Dakar, Senegal
New York, New York

Contact publisher's representative Dustin Pickering:
publication.worldinkers@gmail.com

ISBN-13: 978-2-487017-05-4

LIGHT INSPIRED

a novel by
Anuradha Bhattacharyya

<u>Other works by this author:</u>

Poetry

Corona Doldrums (New Delhi: Authors Press 2021)
My Dadu (New Delhi: Adhyaya Books 2020)
Lofty – to fill up a cultural chasm (Kolkata: Writers Workshop 2015)
Knots (Kolkata: Writers Workshop 2012)
Fifty-Five Poems (Calcutta: Writers Workshop 1998)

Novels

Jadu (New Delhi: Authors Press 2021)
Still She Cried (New Delhi: Authors Press 2019)
One Word (New Delhi: Creative Crows Publishers 2016)
The Road Taken (New Delhi: Creative Crows Publishers 2015)

Academic Works

Twentieth Century European Literature – a cultural baggage (New Delhi: Creative Crows Publishers 2016)
The Lacanian Author (Chandigarh: Kafla Intercontinental 2015)

Contents

Introduction

I N THIS UNIQUE journey called writing, there are several stations, stopping by which one can pick up a few grains of wisdom. As the journey progresses, the experiences of those stoppages conjoin to yield special insights. The trick for success in writing is to linger on those experiences even after you have departed the station.

Writing is a special vehicle for sharing one's accumulated wisdom, bit by bit, or fictionally put together in a single story. I am sharing here a story that is inspired by the life and thoughts of a young man named Deep Narayan Nayak, whom I came to know a few months ago.

The core of his wisdom is to illuminate many hearts through his tireless striving. His is a story of how light can be kindled from a struggle with shadows. The shadow he had dealt with, in his childhood, empowered him to identify similar shadows in other human beings. Not only that, he also came across worse than shadows – complete darkness.

I have been awestruck by the way he speaks about the villages he has worked for. He has infinite respect for all creatures. From the shadows of ignorance, when he draws them to light, he is not watching his steps. He goes headlong into what he thinks is necessary. Thankfully, he is blessed with the instinct for the right path.

He calls his endeavour, the teacher of the streets. He invites his fellow men to act as he does. He has spread the message in remote districts of India, places where political interference is the least. According to me, his motto is, I go where political leaders fear to tread.

Looking back at the type of government intervention designed to bring to light all the backward classes, I feel, for all these seventy-five years, they have done very little. Their minions are insincere. Even some of the local orders are directly opposite of what makes the poor enlightened.

Ignoring all hurdles and taking many risks, Nayak has made great strides in educating backward classes. I told him, poverty is a favourite subject of writers. He was not amused. He has seen so much poverty that what the fictionists have written appears far less dismal.

His enthusiasm for the Adivasi community, which is his focus now, prodded me to look at education from a philosophical perspective. I am not very comfortable telling tales of squalid situations, but I decided to delve on the mystic quality of his efforts. In this narrative, fictionally told by his eldest sister, I have omitted references to places, time, the pandemic and other circumstantial facts that probably enhanced his philanthropy. The guiding principle of this litany is educationist. The guiding light is the man I am calling Deepu.

Anuradha Bhattacharyya
Chandigarh

CHAPTER ONE: FORTUNE

FORTUNE SUFFERS FROM a distinguished form of restlessness. She decides to move in ways utterly strange to humankind. Following her track is impossible. Her scattering tendency has brought many families to extinction. Her waywardness has brought many upright gentlemen to their knees. Fortune disappears like smoke in the clouds. Fortune takes with her your pride, your fame, your dignity. She shatters the crystal sphere of complacency and thrusts you in the vacuum of space where no shuttle can drop you back home. She is illusion. She is delusion. She is corruption. She is annihilation. She is capricious to the core. She does not forgive a mistake. Nor does she reward you for your good. In short, she leaves you as her whim may dictate. She comes to you as whimsically.

Fortune is therefore, untrustworthy. She latches on to an individual for a while, quite irrationally, and some people take her for granted until she is gone as irrationally, and then some people must go fetching her in all sorts of near-death situations. Fortune vanishes from one house and settles in another. In her restlessness, it judges no one. In her caprice, Ma Lakshmi pushes kind people to the fringes of poverty and bestows her blessings on some of the most undeserving.

If I must speak of fortune in this vein, I shall be exhausting the whole story; for, I do have a story to tell. My own as well as that of my grandfather and then, the surprise introduction of my little brother, who, I must confess at the very outset, is destined to be the hero of this particular litany.

*

Ages ago, there were zamindars who acted as overlords for a cluster of villages comprising about a few thousand people, young, old, bald, bearded, clothed, underfed, turbaned or saree-clad. People who could be distinguished as warm hearted, hardworking and enjoying the tilling of the land in the anticipation of rice for the family. The zamindar took the lion's share, as indeed he was the lion who knew how to grab things, tear them away from their rightful owners and feed on them. But when he was satisfied, he wandered around watching genially over his populace, perhaps rendering a short spell of kindness when the occasion arose.

I shouldn't speak too harshly about them. All are human. Humans do have vices. They are social animals who wander about the earth with a greedy belly and a fearful heart. A mix of vices is a blessing for them. Humans have the greatest fortune on this planet, doubtless, with an equal share of responsibility to keep the planet going. To live here is to grab and disseminate alternately. So did my ancestors and by that I mean, those few people whose blood I have inherited, but alas, without the fortune. The burden of responsibility too eased away with that slackening of dignity, the need to hold the head high, and command over a bunch of villagers. In short, it was time to beg.

The British erased most of our traditional systems and grafted some administration that no one understood. Gradually, the hold over the people we loved and relied on loosened and we also had a few back stabbers to blame for this. When it did dawn on us that the wealth we gained from the tilling of our lands was not enough to meet our daily necessities, we sought work in the developing infrastructure that included the building of railways.

My grandfather took up the job of a foreman. A foreman, precisely, was entrusted with overseeing the laying of the railway tracks and then running the locomotive to check if it was neatly done. A heavy thing of the sort can wring your neck if you happen to fall in its tracks. One day my grandfather was lucky enough to have his hands and feet severed under it in one go, and very lucky indeed to have left for the other world in another five days, wasting all his hard-earned blood on the hospital bed. Fortune, as I said, was already turning her face away from us and this was particularly distasteful to her, and so she hastened her departure from our family.

*

My mother was five years old. She told me this little detail from her memory. Her elder brother was ten years old, maturer than her but he never conveyed the details of this little misadventure of my grandfather. All he recalled was the utter distress of the family of four children when the earning member left them in the lurch. The father gone, the breadwinner burned, the hearth doused in water and the roof battered in the rain of tears. Nothing could stir him to sing the litany of his father's departure for me to be able to forward it to you, my readers, with infused pathos that can draw buckets of tears.

A matter of fact that remains remarkable is the loss of fortune. Poverty entered the vicinity of my family like a gnawing rat that could rip off the last vestiges of the zamindari that we owned and left us to beg for work, beg for food, beg for recognition and yes, along with all the beautiful souls that worked towards it, beg for freedom from the British.

If I were to now change the title of my narrative to poverty, with a capital P, I won't be far from the truth. Poverty has held more than half of the attention of my family ever since. Poverty fostered us, kind of. Let's put it this way, poverty is the half sister of fortune that dissolves her beneficence. Fatherless, the boy of fifteen looked for work and was turned away everywhere he went since he was not cut out to be a labourer. He did not qualify as one. He did not fit the definition of worker, such as drones of a bee hive. He was not only too young but also brought up as a gentleman. A boy of gentle manners and kindness. The ones who knew how to work in the fields and break stones or forge iron abhorred him, made fun of him, and never befriended him. The school which he was studying in did not expel him either. He belonged to that class by blood and managed to graduate to the level of being a clerk. Again, how he managed that feat has never been explained to the next generation. We were onlookers of the story that unfolded and were mum about it. Some of us never cared to know our ancestors. Some of us never cared to ask how landlords became landless and some of us even grabbed back a share of our rightless belongings from relatives, and refused to recognize them. The lion's share went back to the lions of the new generation and somehow my uncle and my little mother did not quite fit into that definition either.

She was a happy little girl. Her elder brother was kind and caring. He managed to bring her up like all other normal poor children, no school, no gifts, no finery and no manners. To top it all, she turned out to be the owner of such enormous teeth that could put a bunny to shame. At first it was surmised that when she gained some flesh the teeth would go under. But by the time of her puberty, there was no sign of gaining flesh and the sole power of her growth rested on her enormous teeth.

Uncle had to look for a groom for her. It was necessary to pack her off with a man so that no stray dog might lay his teeth upon her, so to say. Or take it this way, with puberty came the hysteria of women who crave for sex. That's how tradition taught Indians to stash away an eleven-year-old with any man who vows to feed her. Caste, class, wealth factors withstanding, someone did appear on the horizon and though I am proud of him now, at that time he was perhaps the only suitor she could get. My father, who fathered another four children, was a cool gentleman with his own history of wily fortune.

Our father, I should henceforth call him, married my mother at the tender age of fourteen. He too wasn't much of a man then but matched her passably. It was never clear where all the wealth of his zamindari had flown off. But for the moment, he lived in a large house, worked in a chemist's shop and had been to school.

The sprawling bungalow was all that the family could boast of. Inside it was bereft of money, food, comforts, and morals. All lost in the flood of fortune who decided to leave them in the lurch, as she always does with well off people. Sometime back I was told by one of my selfish uncles that fortune decided to flow out of that bungalow soon after my mother arrived there. This uncle of mine was ten years younger to my father and wholly depended on the family at that time. This ungrateful wretch was going to school at my father's expense, ate, slept and played at his mercy and still complained that all went to rot only after my father brought home a wife. The wife's enormous teeth bothered this uncle of mine and he cursed her in his dreams. He must have even schemed against her in his heart so that soon after the wedding, the head of the family fell to coughing and spitting venom all over the house. His coughing was so loud and so incessant that it roused all the ayurvedic doctors in the vicinity. From street to street and from village to village, it became a long struggle to get his coughing under control. This continued for around four years. The man, who was about fifty years old, robust and hearty, gradually dwindled to a clanking skeleton, just skin and bones and a large rib cage for all to learn anatomy.

My uncle had gifted some gold jewelry to my mother on her wedding. She wore the necklace, bangles and a pair of earrings and kept the rest of the precious metal in a large wooden trunk. That's how people kept their wealth in those days. And in our family, a woman's dowry is all hers. She keeps it in her bedroom and can decide when to touch it. With that bundle of gold jewelry my uncle had wagered a skinny girl with protruding teeth to a large happy family. You can add the golden heart in her bosom too. It did not show up at once but gradually, when the patriarch shrunk into a coughing bundle of bones, her little stock of gold began to shine in everybody's eyes.

An x-ray in the city hospital proved it to be tuberculosis. TB, in those days was unmanageable. It could be contracted. It could be suppressed with warmth or it could be left to take its course. TB decided to stay put in the old man's lungs. There were no antibiotics in the human world. The lion of the planet had not yet discovered it. Begrudgingly, the family tended the dwindling old patriarch and awaited the last call.

My father lit the funeral pyre and was entitled to act as the next patriarch. He had to pay his respects to the forefathers and seek their blessings through the ritual of shraddh. The first-born son has no choice. He is the karta of the family when his father dies. He cannot get away from his duties but no one perceives him as overburdened. Everyone thinks of him as the privileged one. The karta is the one who performs all the duties of the head of a family. My father brought up the rest of the four children as if they were his own. He and my mother became the sole provider for them. They didn't even get anything cherishable from it.

*

Once the little ones completed school and fetched some work, my parents decided to walk out of their lives, walk out of the bungalow which was a constraint now and settle somewhere else. The idea was to keep the family small and limit the family needs to themselves and their offspring.

Poverty, the half-sister of fortune, never quit their side. She walked out of the bungalow and settled on the roof of my parents' one thousand square feet plot in the midst of an unkempt fruit orchard. This particular orchard was owned by my father's uncle, someone who lived far away from the patriarchal bungalow, ostensibly because he did not wish to be a burden on his father. This was possible because he was the second son, not the first. So, there were no obligations on him to belong. He had persisted in his studies during the brighter years of zamindari. He had taken to looking after a warehouse and was paid handsomely.

Now look at how fortune works. My father's uncle was wealthy but he had only two eyes and two feet and two hands and well, one stomach and one heart and nothing monstrous or divine about him. His wealth needed more hands, more legs, more eyes, more lungs and perhaps it would be wrong to say that it needed more hearts as you might mistake it for some intention to plunder. But he definitely was alone. What went wrong with his family planning; I am not the right person to comment on that. However, he had a heart large enough to accommodate my entire family: my father, mother and us three sisters.

It was philanthropy. He gave my father the job of gatekeeper. My mother spontaneously became the housekeeper and we three sisters got to go to school. Grand, isn't it?

This grand uncle of mine travelled a lot. He left his house to our care and went about with his business in cities. We had a good shelter and enough water and enough breezes in the summers. We got enough warmth in the winters. We had good mosquito nets during the monsoons. There was electricity, tap water and if it failed, ground water to pump out. There was a kitchen garden that we all tended and two little pups whom we reared. There was an abundance of space, clothing, and a lot of free time to listen to music. We could walk a few kilometres to reach the railway station near which the yearly haat was held. There we found little trumpets, drums and a clay bird that we could whistle.

It lasted till I turned ten.

Fortune was becoming a habit in our family and it had to be broken. Grand uncle turned grey and balding. His legs creaked when he walked and he felt insecure in his travels. He finally decided to settle back at home.

When he stayed with us, there were a few disagreements. He did not want us to laugh loudly. We children started living in the other end of the bungalow. He did not like the fries my mother cooked. He thought of keeping a hired cook. He did not like the kind of songs we played on the radio so we lost its use. Gradually, my father began to offer advice to him, considering him an old man.

Between them it was finally decided that the patron did not need us anymore. He presented us with a thousand square feet plot in the middle of his neglected orchard and said it was upon us how we organised the place. It was only the plot. The mud house we built on it was a small sustainable room and the first thing I cried out about was the lack of electricity. Then it dawned upon me that we would have to fetch water from a long distance away. It infuriated us to find out that from now on all of us would be sleeping on the floor together.

It was still very much an adventure for us. The building of the mud house with loose bricks bought from the market, the clay tiles that clattered if you dropped them, the tiny square windows my father made from wood from the trees and the great porch in the front where all the pots and pans were piled up. We were to start early in the morning to fetch water from the nearest well and come home to cook food in the open. That was why the porch was carefully made. The tiles covered the porch as well, giving the hut the look of low ceiling.

In about five months into this little house of ours, my mother showed signs of being pregnant. She spewed her breakfast a few times, refused to eat fish and also neglected housekeeping. My sisters and I gradually took up as much housework as were possible for kids. My younger sister was very conscientious about cleanliness. She neglected her homework to do housework. I did the cooking in the morning and evening. We were quite happy. My father went to work in a chemist's shop as a handyman and returned home late. On Mondays, he did enough tending of the back and sides of the house so that we could grow local tomatoes. When tomatoes grew in abundance in the monsoons, we passed our days having only tomato and potato gravy.

Capricious fortune had stealthily left us and we were only lately realising the effect. We had constructed our new home in February. It was dry and windy so we needed neither a mosquito net nor a fan. We lacked electricity but because we rose early in the morning to finish all the chores before leaving for school, we got tired by sunset and did not complain about going to bed early.

The first stormy night was an awakening. We realised how vulnerable our situation had become. First, the trees swayed frighteningly. Monstrous shadows peeped in through the tiny window and moaned with anticipation. They seemed to warn us not to speak and betray our presence otherwise they were going to get us, sweep us off our feet and hurl us down with a smash in the white slimy sands of the seashore. Then came the peeling thunderclap. It was the end of April and all the bright stars had gone off to some distant land, abandoning the planet to the nasty onslaught of a monster. The monster yelped, screamed, wailed, growled, rumbled, and threatened us as if we were the only ones he could spy upon in the eternal dimness that the sky had left us in. The deserted sky moaned and gasped and flung its arms to get back its stars. The black trees shrieked in pain as they were thrust from one end to another like a broom that the monster did not know how to use.

Two days of non-stop storm revealed all the vulnerabilities of our new home and on the third day we took on the task of repairing all the broken spots. It was a prelude to the monsoons of June and July. May was a quiet month by comparison. We only had difficulty tending to the plants that we had sown in April. Some of the vegetables needed a lot of water.

The monsoon rains trampled many plants like a wild elephant trying to dance to a rapid beat. The unstoppable torrents that we had relished on paddy fields now appeared to be ill omens. We could not get much from the kitchen garden apart from tomatoes. My father even designed a shelter for the okra plants with intertwined wild vines pulled down from the barren fruit trees. He found plain land where the sun shone for about eight hours in the day. But the same barren land suffered the hardest of slashes when it rained.

Our tiled roof drummed on all night making it impossible for us daughters to fall asleep. In our tired minds we tried to call out to Rama as our mother had taught us to do, to be able to fall asleep. In our tired minds, not only did our own voices sound distant, the image of the Lord took myriad shapes and rather frightened us when the sky cracked.

When it did not rain, mosquitoes came in hordes. We had hand fans made of Sal leaves. Each girl took turns to fan for all three. When one sister's hand slowed down, the next girl snatched the fan from her and fanned with vigour. Nothing helped to get rid of the mosquitoes though. These were large junglee mosquitoes that had fangs as thick as needles. Their buzz was loud and they died in one tiny smash. We had soft little palms and each time we made a kill, the palms were smeared with blood. Having nothing else around us, the most natural tendency was to wipe it on the mat we slept on. Junglee mosquitoes are not acquainted with the habits of humans. They come very close to the eyes, attracted by our breath. In the bungalow, mosquitoes were smaller and smarter, as you know, and weren't easy to smash.

Apart from mosquitoes, we feared scorpions. But it was only a fear. In all those years, our mother insisted much on cleanliness only out of the fear of scorpions. She insisted on keeping her baskets raised up. Most of our belongings would hang from the roof, tied to ropes around the bamboo beams.

The entire room was our bed. It was cast with a thick layer of clay over bricks. It needed touch-ups in scorching heat whereas in the wet season, it remained smooth. And rather ruddy. We sprawled all over the place sticking our sweaty legs even out of the mats and also into the ribs of our siblings. At one point after midnight, after we had heard the boom of a distant iron factory, after we were sure that it was too late, we dropped the Sal fans and gave in to the rumbling music of the sky.

There were beautiful little animals around the place, those that we identified from our book of alphabets and rhymes. The most frequent visitor was a red little fox. My mother said that it came looking for meat. It had a tiny body but a large mouth and a bushy tail. It must have been feeding on rats because we saw many of them scurrying about in the undergrowth. There were hares also but rarely did they come near us. We could see them turn their ears and the glint of their large eyes suddenly in the sun between the foliage but they darted far away from us. Small hedgehogs showed up after the rains, scurrying for food. There were hundreds of monkeys. We initially thought there was only one family and decided to name each individual that was identifiable. Afterwards, we figured out that we had been naming several of them that were indistinguishable.

Monkeys were not afraid of humans. They came very close and bared their teeth. At first, we stood stunned and dropped our glass of water or the banana we were eating. Later on, we learned to hide our belongings. Monkeys made no distinction between edibles and underwear. They screeched and jumped about with a loud clatter on our red tiled roof. It was not possible to frighten them away. We were a single family and a single hut in the wilderness. The village was half a kilometre away.

There was no paved road to the village. On the other end of the orchard ran a lone railway track where we counted just three trains running during the day and none at all in the night. Beyond the village were fields and then another cluster of houses. Those houses were well built but none of them was a bungalow. They had electricity and we learned by and by that if people of this village could pursue the officials to connect a line with that village, we too would get electricity. But this village lacked that kind of leadership until the hero of this tale attained manhood.

Fortune distanced herself from us until then.

*

She definitely has no heart. I finished school using borrowed books and a slate. I walked two kilometres everyday to the school. My immediate sister came along on most of the days but lacked the energy to maintain discipline. She bunked a few classes and was discouraged most of the time. She kept in tow with me on four of the days of the week and remained at home on the other two. Although she learned things fast and found studies easy, there was a lack of determination to pursue the letters. She tried her hand at cooking and did appreciably. I was determined to bring home some money. My father continued as the trusted handyman of the medicine shop to which he went very early by train. He too walked two kilometres. I could see his shop from the porch of my school. Fortune tried us with a blow when that shopkeeper died of liver damage. My father had seen the health of his employer deteriorating. He mentioned it to me and had asked me to keep it to myself. He and I often called out to Ma Durga to keep him well, for our sake indeed. Fortune did not like our selfish prayers. She struck us with a slap on the face and made us look further. She wanted me to work, I guessed; and, made it clear to my father that I loved teaching little children. I said I could teach the alphabet to six-year-olds in the village. We tried to get some family to accept my tutorship but in this village it was impossible. They had no money to spare.

My father refused to send me to unknown homes in the village across the fields. Instinctively, my younger sister suggested that she could do housework for others in this village and make some money so that I could join college and become a better teacher. She said that as a didi, I was more likely to be able to shoulder the burden in another three years with a handsome salary after graduation whereas, her being too young, graduation for her was a long way off. It was sound advice coming from the brightest of us.

I promised myself that three years later, she would resume her studies. She was very good and got such good grades in school that giving up her schooling was a scandal. My mother was the most unhappy. The proposed idea was to let her go to wash utensils and clothes in other households of the village. It infuriated my mother. She relented for a month and waited for my father to find another job. But he had grown grey and thin. The initial youthfulness of his limbs had given way to gout. He was over forty but looked nearly fifty. No one took him in. He walked over to the railway officers' colony far off, a few times to get work as a coolie, or a gardener, but everyone turned him away. Finally, he resigned to tilling the little kitchen garden we had. He expanded it and also went into the orchard to look after some of the fruit bearing trees such as guava. He tried to free them of the climbers and bring them back to bloom.

My younger sister was energetic and soon found kind people in the neighbourhood where she worked. They gave her their leftovers to eat and she even brought home a few goodies when they had a puja at home. In those two years that she worked for others, my immediate sister continued with her schooling and I went to study Bangla in a college. I walked to the station, took a train and then walked to the college. The whole trip took me two hours. The return journey was also the same except that if I could take an early train, I made it home before nightfall.

It was a pious activity. We were all very sad and we wanted more money every other day. We had a ration card with our names printed on it, duly stamped by the municipality. We received the ration once a month and finished it in half months' time. After that we depended on what my younger sister brought in charity. That lack was replenished again in the next month and again we starved at the end of it. It kept us going.

One day, we had no more kerosene. My sister happened to mention this bit of hardship to the matron of the family she was working for. She offered her share of the kerosene on the condition that her pay would be reduced. My sister consulted us at home and agreed to the condition because the ten rupees that was reduced did not add up to the price of the one Litre kerosene that she was getting. But we kept that kerosene for emergencies and stopped lighting a lamp after sunset. It affected our studies to some extent but I managed to read a little on the train.

In the passenger trains we do not always get a seat. I used to hold the overhead ring with my right arm and the open book in front of me with the left palm. Many people saw this as a routine and offered me a seat, especially the elderly women. I believe, in every heart there must be a spot left vacant with the desire to be learned. Sacrificing a piece of comfort for the next generation is a supremely human instinct.

Fortune turned her face back towards us when my sister saw the shop open again. She came home and encouraged her father to accompany her to the school the next day and see for himself. He went reluctantly but seeing him, the son of the chemist, who was now opening a confectionary shop, brightened up. He was rather glad to have a trustworthy helping hand from his father's time as an employee. We thanked Ma Durga.

In another year, I was a graduate. I started reading the newspaper for advertisements. I was ready for anything, from a typist to a tailor but at the back of my head throbbed the only sentiment I always nourished – teaching. Soon I found a job as an Anganwadi worker. We thanked our good fortune and I was about to send my younger sister back to school when new trouble cropped up.

*

She was too beautiful to be spared.

That little bundle of flesh, wrapped in a blue kurti and churidar that was gifted to her affectionately by our uncle, drew the longing gaze of a sourly gentleman. He was morose and all alone among a host of cantankerous sisters. He was the third child in the family, the only son to have survived typhoid and therefore, much attended to. All that attention made him morose, for reasons unknown to me. I saw him only when he came with his father to our house, asking for her hand. We were utterly confused. What had she done?

My cousin's wedding was an occasion for a happy reunion of kith and kin. My mother could not take all of us to the ceremony at once. My father and I stayed back while my two sisters and Deepu went with her, two days before the wedding day. We joined them only on the wedding day. There were many guests among whom, a gentleman found her charming. He was thirty years old and was a little weak for a man. He needed a thoughtful and wise woman for a wife. He was not particularly after money, so we would be spared the trouble of giving a dowry. To my uncle, he expressed his desire to marry my sister so he was given our address. We had never quite thought of her in those lines. She had been supporting the family and we were speechless when it crossed our mind that that support would be gone.

I was four months into the job at the Anganwadi centre. I had not saved a single penny. I bought utensils, dresses and spent on repair work in the house. Now, all of a sudden the unexpected prospect of arranging a wedding ceremony overwhelmed me. Hard as it may sound, the thought of her schooling just vanished from my mind. Not even for a second did I see schooling as more important than finding a groom. I spent one little sleepless night contemplating the marriage and decided it was a blessing.

She was still a child. She started lisping, like a frightened parrot. She stopped smiling and went about with a pout. I bought her pink lipstick. She put it aside. She wanted to know what it would entail. My mother spent a little while explaining the possibilities but she was not convinced. She turned to me and asked things I was very shy to tell her. It was a jumble and mumble and all in vain.

She was then only sixteen and I was aware of the fact that the legal marriageable age was eighteen for a girl. I was aware that the limit of eighteen was a wise decision, as it was after finishing school. But all of literature is filled with sweet sixteen. Most of the fiction on blooming love relationships described the sixteen-year-old girl as most beautiful, most desirable and probably sweet, chubby, and cuddly for a man. Not much was clear about health and fertility except that kissing was enjoyable.

Kissing the pout that she carried around at the thought of marriage.

My mother wanted to see the home she would go to. So, she went out one day and had a look at it. Not that it was very clear at the outset that that home would keep her daughter happy. Many intrigues take place in the innards of a household. Once the child is swallowed into it, the household closes up again. The outward pomp and show last only a fortnight. The entrails of a household may be rotten but the world never gets a whiff of it. Sometimes there are rumours of some part of a family having lost its credibility, but unless you are a participant in the very system, you can't point a finger at the exact rotten part. Worse than that, even if you are a member, it is next to impossible to expel that rotten part. My mother's visit was a formality, that's all.

Fortune had her say in it. She decided for us, all that we learned gradually. She decided who would be happy and who would wait to be happy next month. I prayed to Ma Durga to keep my sweet sister happy. I told her that she was fortunate that she wouldn't be working in other people's homes for any longer. I forgot to tell her that I was planning to send her to school to complete her studies. Now, on reflection, I can reason that the last resort still would have been a marriage. In our society, no one is allowed to remain single for long. Not even a wage earner. Not even a beggar, I should say. Girls in particular have to be tied to a pole, so to say, around which her dreams and aspirations and all her activities revolved. Never ever can she be allowed to venture far out of the circle of that pole's shadow. So, fortune's dictate in my sister's case was rather welcomed by all of us.

When she left us, the gap was immediately filled up by my immediate sister. By then she had finished school and was left free to tend to the household. She even acted as mother to the toddler we had by now. And yes, that toddler is the hero of my litany, I must remind you. And I am not sharing much about it at present because my tryst with fortune is not over yet.

*

The wedding ceremony involved over one hundred people. All the villagers were invited. All the villagers of the groom's family were also invited. Not only them, my father came up with a list of all sorts of strangers naming them as family. I heard tales of men and women whom I had never seen. Those relatives lived scattered over all of North 24 Parganas and I had never ever visited them. My father too had not visited many of them and did not know their proper names or if the number of members in their family had grown. He just knew that they were family and therefore, deserved an invitation.

For many days and nights, he travelled to places by train or by bus to distribute sweets and an invitation letter. It turned out that they, most of them, did not take that much pain to return the visit on the wedding day. In the future, likewise, though many invitations to weddings came our way too, we offered our prayers to Ma Durga in our hearth, calmly avoiding the obligation to attend. Well, that way, my sister did receive a hundred or more blessings. Altogether, it was part of our duty to let people far and wide know that she was duly married and settled with so and so in such and such a village.

The wedding days were arduous. It was fixed in the middle of April and the days were very hot. My wedding was slaughtered by the monsoons and I have no qualms in saying that I was rather glad. In her case, I was sweaty and panting with the running about and with no one actually to do the menial jobs around the home; it was a very nasty affair. All the cleaning, brushing and counting fell on us. Some villagers helped with the decoration and fetching things from the market, but that was help for my father, not us. We continued on our own, the flooring and the alpana, the scrubbing and the mending, the counting of gifts for the groom's family and always reminding father to bring yet another thing, it was plain insanity. Nothing can be perfect in such situations. The guests would still have something to dislike, something to make a face about and then go back to their village and speak ill of ours. I think it is herd instinct, but surely, mankind should learn to feel for a bigger herd.

My sister's saree was a bright red silk. It is impossible to keep it in good condition on the wedding day. The girl was sweating all over and on top of that the flower garland oozed messily on her bosom. The hair pinned up painfully in a bun where her hair was hardly long. The rajanigandha wreath around her bun and the net veil on top of it suffocated her. We made her sit on a stool for the greater part of the day until the groom arrived. Then they had to sit cross-legged on a mat. We fanned her incessantly and wiped her face with a gamchha. Afterwards we gave her a white towel to hold.

Starved and hot and dizzy, my sister looked hardly appealing in that wedding dress. But we were very jovial all day. The groom was very jovial, although initially, we had found him haughty. He kept darting his smiling glance at her face with satisfaction. He did look like a man looking forward to a happy life.

We all knew that the ritual of a wedding was an offering in prayer for blessings from the forefathers and Lord Narayana. The offerings to the fire god were an appeal for purity and sanctity. The offerings to the other gods were appeals towards safety and longevity. All in all, the groom was the main supplicant and we were the onlookers. The priest was a guide but hardly mattered if he faltered. The groom and the bride were fasting and praying for their future together and vows or no vows, wishes or no wishes, it was generally understood that they would procreate and share the burden of responsibilities together for the rest of their lives, whether they liked it or not, whether they were fed up of it or just wanted to let go, whether they cared for each other or not. Fortune, as always, would not depend on their intentions but on their luck. If she willed, she would bless them and if she was sly, she would play hide and seek with them as she was wont to.

Weeping is customary. Not every family imagines that the daughter will be treated as a slave in the other home but definitely, she will not be by our side on every occasion. She will have to surrender her will to the dictates of the other house where, in particular, the elders lived. Most homes are joint homes. Most people resent a split in attention and worse so, some people look at it as a departure from loyalty if the girl attaches too much importance to the affairs of her father's home. Freedom to follow her heart is restricted. I don't know much of that because I married quite late in my life and I left the in-laws pretty early. But she lived quite satisfactorily with her in-laws. At least that's what is reported. What goes in the bowels of a system cannot be comprehended from the outside.

Many years later, I saw a gold bangle on her wrist along with her shankha-pola. I was dazzled by it. She always wore good cotton sarees and shapely blouses. She had two sons and a daughter and she seemed to have had enough to eat as she had developed a liking for betel leaves. Betel chewing is a sign of wellbeing. I have even received a saree from her on Durga Puja that looked like silk. Though, I have never gifted her anything other than sweets.

*

My immediate sister contracted malaria soon after the wedding. As I said, poverty was the half-sister of fortune. She just barged in, grabbed all our assets, and would not budge. She stuck about as if she belonged, as if she liked us. What could she like about us when we were so peeved, so miserable, so soured by her presence? Yet she stayed. We tended to my sister like worn out rabbit furs. We had no flesh. We dumped blankets on her body and had no mattress to spread underneath. She shivered all along. We did not know what else to do and because it was malaria, we merely administered the medicine. There was no milk, no meat, no tonic that could have quickened her recovery. We waited and we waited day in and day out. We just sat next to her and put a hand on her head. She even removed the hand explaining that it felt heavy on her forehead. But because we wanted to touch her somewhere, we then chose a foot or her knee and it always caused her pain. Humankind has been at war with mosquitoes since prehistoric times and still we have not won.

Malaria isn't the only malaise over here. There're lice in the hair and we are pretty fond of keeping long hair. Then there's that awful bed bug. Thank goodness, we had no beds. We only had the kantha spread on the mat. And it was all right during the summers because a mattress gathers heat. We longed to have a cot. The rope-cot is even more comfortable in summers as it does not trap any body heat. It follows our curves and it leaves our body dry from underneath as well. But the bed bug clung to our kantha like family. It was our blood.

Usually, neem oil helps to remove lice. Women don't get to shave off their hair unless, as in some parts of India, it's a condition of widowhood. We arduously applied coconut oil and scratched and scratched our heads furiously. And there's never an escape because the whole family that ate together and slept together on the same floor daily was infected all at once.

But scratching actually reminds me of our hero. The one who came into my mother's womb soon after we left the large bungalow of my grand uncle was no other than the presumptuous hero of my litany. And with him, I felt in those days, poverty, the half-sister of fortune seized her place.

*

Many years after his arrival, I came to know from my mother that she had prayed to Ma Kali for the boon of a son. It explained why she would weep in the daytime while cooking rice and watching the little boy scratching all over his body, screwing up his face in pain and irritation and intermittently, calling out Ma. She was actually, no, really, in earnest, praying to Ma Kali. I am sure she was coaxing a promise from Ma Kali that the boy would live. Fervently, when he had arrived that night, my mother had felt a bright light engulf her being, and she was filled with contentment. That's when she called her Deepu and then on, we have been calling him Deepu, meaning the light of her prayers, the fulfillment of her wish to give birth to a son.

It is said that the son is the only source of release from this mortal world. If the son offers his respects to the departed souls of the parents, the souls go straight to heaven and do not wander about as spirits around the offspring.

We sisters knew that belief very well. We had seen people go crazy in prayers asking for a son but that such a craze rocked the bosoms of our parents too had not crossed our minds. We whispered to each other that the boy was malaise embodied. He puked and he went for the runs after almost every meal. We were made doubly busy after his birth. Washing, cleaning, scrubbing, and bathing. The only solace was that he came in the month of March. It was neither too cold nor wet. He could survive all the bathing that we administered him.

We took turns. The main sentiment was to help our mother. We needed her, not him, but for her sake we fed Deepu, we cleaned Deepu's waste, we wrapped up Deepu in our old cotton frocks and we also laughed and giggled when he was irked.

When mother recovered strength, she took him to uncle's house and showed him off like a new found gem. We were very jealous. But we had nothing to say about him because he was already proving to be a huge trouble to our parents, the huge unwanted trouble that Ma took for a blessing.

It was about two in the morning when he popped out of mother's womb along with a rush of water. My father had heard her groan and went out to call the midwife. Meanwhile, the head had popped out and we had to hold a bowl under him. The midwife came and pulled the rest of him out and cleaned him, held him upside down and he squealed all right. I thought of it as a major success, conscious of the fact that I was also a woman and someday I would also be sprawled naked before the family and deliver a baby. I was conscious that it would be painful but I'd smile and I'd express more concern about the health of the baby than my own bleeding.

All that and many more unpleasant things associated with motherhood registered in my mind when Deepu came. At the age of three he was up to endless mischief. One day he drank a whole vial of homoeopathic medicine that was meant for my father. It was felt as a loss of one year's medicine at first until Deepu developed unfamiliar rashes.

Fortune's half-sister reared her sinister head and almost threatened us with more tragic prospects. While all three of us were skinny and dirty, there was hardly any sign of sickness in the family. At least there was nothing life threatening. With Deepu, it was always an extreme kind of problem. If he had dysentery, it was like water. If Deepu had vomiting, it was an upturning of his bowels with loud howls and tears and pee and everything unpleasant that we girls never made our parents go through.

On his eleventh birthday, he suddenly started haranguing father about holding a party. Other mothers, he had felt, cooked kheer on the anniversary of their child's birth and invited all the neighbouring children to a feast. It was, I knew, an offering in prayer, an offering to the gods in children to keep their own child healthy and happy. It was, I knew, a superstition, starting with the visit to the Shiva temple in the morning and keeping a vegetarian diet all day, leaving a lighted lamp on the pooja rack. If she cooked a lot of kheer and distributed puri and aloo-dum to other children in the likeness of a celebration, she gave her own child a happy day.

Deepu understood it otherwise. He started out by complaining that he was obliged to pay back that treat. He had visited homes, helped himself to the generous feast and now, those neighbourhood kids should also be served at his home on his birthday. Mother did everything else, starting with the visit to the Shiva temple, keeping a fast and lighting a lamp, but the kheer was unaffordable.

As his birthday was approaching, he asked mother to invite his friends. Mother refused to do so. He went out and told all his friends that it was his birthday next Monday. He went about hinting that there might be a party at his place and all would be invited. As a result, the neighbours flashed broad smiles at all of us for no reason we could fathom.

On Saturday, he got restless and spewed out a few cruel words. It expressed the sentiment that we were not doing enough for his prestige. Poverty comes with the condition that we would be bereft of prestige. We must beg, borrow, or steal to make ends meet. Though we were grateful that we were working, much of our food and clothes came in charity, which we paid back for by sacrificing our sense of prestige.

My mother at last lost her temper and dealt him a tight slap. I rushed to pull the boy out of her reach, but he was heavy by then and sprang up to his feet. With the swing of his bony hand he tried to push me away and I fell to the floor, scattering some of the pots. Mother screamed at him and used both of her hands to slap him on the legs and buttocks and tears rolled down her cheeks.

My father was returning home at that time and from the street, heard the commotion, and picked up pace. Upon entering the house, he saw me and mother sprawled on the floor screaming indistinctly and Deepu standing erect in the middle, arms akimbo. He lost his voice and asked in one word, 'what', so Deepu began his harangue once again. He had hoped that father would comply. He thought that perhaps father would see the situation from his angle. He did not know him to be unreasonable. He was an affectionate father. So, he said everything that he had already been saying to mother.

Mother and I got up and sat cross-legged on the floor. We watched him and father warily. We did not interject. What followed was completely unexpected. Father went out, quite calmly, as if he had gone to open up a pit of treasure to hand over to us. Deepu rested his butt on the iron trunk. He seemed to be satisfied with his arguments, his eyebrows screwed up as if reconsidering if it was foolish to approach the women at the outset. His hands rested on the trunk, expressing his confidence.

My father had gone out to fetch a stick. He entered with the stick poised for attack. Upon his lips were the words, 'is that why you hit your mother?'

We sisters felt proud and content to think that we were much better than Deepu.

CHAPTER TWO: HEALTH

HEALTH AND FITNESS find place in common mind only after the three basic necessities, food, shelter and clothing are met. Health is gay. He loves only his own kind. Health befits the company of the already healthy. Health seeks refuge in healthy homes. Health steals away from the homes with deficiencies. Health is narcissistic. Health refers to the mirror to decide what to love. Health packs his bags and walks out of your doors if you can't show up another healthy body as consort.

Health is so attractive that it is not only difficult to resist, but also impossible to ignore. You may think that you'd smile at the thought of health and that would be enough. You may think that health is partying, and your saying hello to him would be enough. You may think that health visited you in the middle of the night, climbed into your room through the window and seeing you fast asleep, was satisfied. So you don't need to pay attention to him. So you don't need to pamper him with tonics, pills and lotions. So you don't need to filter the water that you drink. So you don't need to sterilise your napkins. So you don't need to powder your sores. You don't need to test your blood for bacteria.

The water that you drink is the reflection of the condition of your health. Health will keep you happy if you drink filtered water. Health will become very demanding. Health will keep troubling you if you drink tap water, the water that runs several kilometres through the pipes from the treatment plants to your homes. Health will keep troubling you with the warning that it's not safe, but you drink it. It carries pathogens, but you drink it. It will make you sick but you drink it as it will increase your immunity. Health will love you for your health. Health will not allow you to fall sick with tap water. He will hug you tight and allow you to fall peacefully asleep while your blood does the filtering. That's how health will lead you from struggle to success, from disease to cure, from rashes to clear skin and from throwing up to thriving.

*

Yes, most of what Deepu ate was thrown up. When exactly, he would befriend health, was a growing concern in the family. On top of that, he was a huge chatterbox. Whatever he learned from the outside world, he threw that up as well. He would be teaching mother how to clip her toenails, for instance. Now, at that age and in those days of turmoil, whoever thought of clipping one's nails? There were very many other important things to do. But since Deepu saw someone do it, he had to pester mother with the thought. And what vocabulary! He knew nothing! He had to manage with jerky limbs and gawky gestures and inadequate words to formulate the rite of toenail management.

Later on, I realised that toenails did not quite grow long. They fell off along with minor cuts and wounds on the feet because we wore chappals. It is imperative to clip one's toes for those who wear shoes. But following Deepu's instructions my father happened to bring home a nail-cutter that was definitely hard on the budget.

We used our father's discarded blades to cut the finger nails. Earlier, he used to go to the barber and got all the grooming done for one season. We made fun of him but he demonstrated its use by cutting his finger nails for the first time with the device.

Health also has an alter-ego in the form of allergy. Allergies show up on the frontiers of sickness. Before making us fall headlong into the quagmire of disease, allergies warn us and give us a chance to attack the filthy thing before it takes root in our body. This was what Deepu demonstrated to the fullest.

We took him to the homoeopath, not knowing that the cure would last ages. The homoeopath examined his teeth and gums, his eyes and ears, the texture of his hair and interrogated him and my mother for an hour. My mother was breathless at last. Timidly, she told the homoeopath that she had housework to do and he must hurry up with the diagnosis.

Well, there are only three homoeopathy medicines in the whole world: one for cough, one for sunburn and one for the skin.

Sunburn is easily cured by covering the skin altogether. However, homoeopathic medicines help somewhat. Skin rashes from allergies due to food or clothing can be attended to by homoeopathic ways. Cough is easily treated by the homoeopaths if you consult them very early. They can't save your lungs if those are infected but they can remove the initial irritation in the nose and throat, especially if it's a child's.

My mother knew no other doctor in the vicinity. She took Deepu to the homoeopath, handed him ten rupees and brought home a vial of tiny white sugar drops. The medicine had been mixed in them. Deepu scratched and scratched all over his body. He looked tremendously ugly. His four milk teeth at the front were protruding as he had taken after our mother and the skin growing now white, now, red, and now scaly yellow made him look like a little midget.

The sap that oozed out of his open blisters was a sticky transparent liquid that dirtied the kantha. And it was not water-soluble. My father solved our dilemma by bringing home large banana leaves which we spread on his mat. He lay on them, now groaning, now whimpering, and always refusing to eat. If he was forced, he threw up. If we gave him milk, he had loose motions. It was just not going right with his health.

*

My first Anganwadi posting was in a village ten kilometres away from home. I used to take a bus and reach there in half an hour. From the bus stop I had to walk a few metres before reaching the exact location for their teaching. The aim was always the health of children but the audience was inevitably their mothers. The supplication was to get the parents to know how to take care of their little ones.

All that was fine with me. What went wrong for me was the constitution of the village. More than half of the population was lepers. Leprosy is such a disease that one can actually carry on without complaint. You can see your fingers wearing out at a rapid speed but you don't feel the pain. Half of the time you just swing in the pleasant numbness of the limbs. You can pinch your skin and not feel a thing. It was quite an attractive idea until your nose got disfigured or when you could not find a life partner.

I had to teach the women to take their medicines regularly. The treatment was free but the regularity could only be maintained if the patients knew for how long it was required. Many patients left off after a couple of months. I had to speak to them like a didi. The teachers are all called didimoni. During my training, I was told that my job was to make the villagers aware of nutrition and primary health care. That I would be posted in an area where a contagious disease was rampant was never clear to me. Afterwards when I sought a transfer, I was told that most of the Anganwadi workers encountered villages of that kind only.

It wasn't the same thing as going to college.

It was just the opposite of health. Health always sought the cleaner areas, away from filth and disease. Health is what we work for. We want to bring home money to cater to our health. When father bought a nail-cutter, he was introducing an element of health in our household. When I made money, I was supposed to introduce mosquito nets. And we always waited for the day when we could bring home a rope-cot. But, to my dismay, I was working in constant fear of contracting a disease.

Health's only way of entry into our household was, as I could perceive at that time, through selfless service to the lepers.

But there were not just women. Women were calm and obedient. They meant to be obedient even if they understood only a fraction of what I said to them. I knew that form of elementary teaching. A teacher has to repeat the same thing a hundred times, the same thing every day until the pupils come up with a question. As long as they are quietly sitting there cross-legged, with faces dedicatedly turned up to you standing in front of them under a massive banyan tree, you can safely assume that they haven't understood a thing. Then you chew your words, break down the syntax and repeat it all in short phrases. It's the time you learn to be a teacher, the pupils not ready yet.

Then one fine day, you get a response for all your efforts. One woman speaks up, usually with an objection to what you've said. That's when you can safely confirm that you have become their teacher.

Primary health care is a project of the government after independence from the British. Otherwise, who cared for health? It was Mother Teresa who transformed her vocation as a Christian Missionary teacher to a service of the poorest of the poor. Still, many people question her methods, as to why she did not hand over many curable patients to general hospitals instead of watching them undergo a slow sad death.

Times were such that the patients overwhelmed the hospitals. Healthcare facilities are supposed to grow in proportion to the growth in population. In a village of five hundred people, one hospital of twenty beds, two thousand people is to eighty beds and so on. But where population growth comes almost free of cost, healthcare facilities require resources at the government level.

I understood that leprosy was one of Mother Teresa's greatest concerns because the lepers enjoyed their benumbed condition. They just begged around, arousing holy horror in the passers-by. They extracted enough money to enjoy life without having to exert themselves. Because, all in all, health requires effort.

The most childish dream of an adult is to become so incapable of work that people would take pity on him and feed him without asking them to repay the kindness. Health runs away from such dreamers. Health abhors lazy people. For food, you must work, for keeping the limbs working, you must exercise, for fitness and bodybuilding, you must do push-ups. For good skin, good hair, good eyes, you must have worked really hard to make that extra money that belongs to health and not just the three basic necessities.

And not surprisingly, the lepers had that pain-free disease that found them food and they asked for nothing else.

Eve teasing: I had only read about it in college. My friends were good people. All of them had come to improve their lives and I did not quite know why so many books are devoted to the subject of eve teasing or molestation and rape. The most common story is always a narrow escape, or an escape with a plan for revenge, or a story of suffering with some divine retribution.

There are also stories of victimizing the victim and then endless conjectures on suicide, fire and stabbing. There are modern day classics on trauma. So, there was a plethora of reading with nil conviction. Unless one has suffered at least a fraction of what it means, there is no conviction about its existence. One feels as if the story is a fantasy that might have gone overboard.

It is more or less like rafting. You read about wild waterfalls and stormy seas and want to go rafting. You can watch films and get excited only to learn afterwards that most of all that was filmed in a studio. So, you do have reason to believe that the writer went overboard when writing about a rape.

In imagination, it is more vicious than what really happens. To normal women, who have those feelers on the skin that signal danger, the situation is tingling, at the most. You just get out of the situation with an involuntary gesture and then reflect on it for hours. A little trauma indeed, but not enough to make you distrust the whole mankind.

After all, one day you too want to bring to the world a little boy.

That's why women are made to forget or not judge the situation too sternly. It's the men folk in the house who worry to the end of the world. My father was never comfortable with the thought of my going to a leper village. Those men with half a finger were aching to touch you. He knew it, but I did not. He knew they would try to sneak up to you by pretending not to be able to speak loudly and then land a peck on your cheek.

I came to know of his fears first and then, after four months of teaching, I faced my first ever misadventure. The skin tingled its signal and I was made aware. My father's voice started speaking inside my head and gradually the disfigured old man crawled up with a whisper on his lips and an erect penis under his lungi. It touched me alright. I cringed. I averted my gaze and tried to come up with a few words. Not to offend the whole population with angry outpours, I ended up apologising to that very old man for my cough and cold and leaving the gathering early.

At home, I told my sister about it. It was the same thing: the need to warn a sister about a danger that she has herself not come across. She listened with attention but quite clearly, did not apprehend the situation as brilliantly as, I am sure, my father did. But I had no intention to tell him about it. I told myself, rather, that such things can be handled discreetly, while keeping my job.

I worked there till the year 2010.

*

Health depends on fortune. These are rungs of a ladder. When Deepu was born, our fortune had gone hurtling down. There was no founding rung to build up health. We sisters often told each other that Deepu did not bring us luck. When he was old enough to talk clearly, he ran off to the wilderness on his own and talked to the birds.

One day he came home wounded by a bird. It was natural, for he had visited their nest. We restricted him for two days until again he ran off, now into the other direction. This time he returned with a puppy. It was sometime in February and the puppy needed shelter. He spent the whole afternoon building a small ante-room for it. My mother had protested that he would dirty the place but she was not aggressive enough. She kept mumbling her protests and it was evident that she did not want to upset her son.

Luckily, Deepu loved cleanliness and therefore, took the puppy into the wilderness for its defecation. We started loving the playful little puppy. Feeding dogs can bring luck. My father got back his job at the shop the very next month. We started rejoicing and loving the puppy even more.

Dogs are associated with wellbeing. It is very easy to preach the benefits of rearing a dog. Dogs are loyal friends and can follow you to places, act as companions and body guards where none of your elder sisters have time to accompany you.

When you are playing with dogs your oxytocin levels increase. You become more empathetic. You can communicate more emotionally with your furry companion than with your mother. You can hug and pet and smother the dog with your love where your elders have no time for you. You can play ball or run about or go for a stroll into strange places when you have all the time in the world and your elder sisters are too tired to go for an adventure.

Caring for a pet reduces anxiety and aggression. Where toddlers are known for their fiery temper, Deepu laughed away care. He would be mischievous and get hurt often but while the dog lasted in our house, he was more intent on taking care of it and forgot many of his maladies.

Playing with pets increases the cardiovascular activities. It strengthens the heart and prepares you for long, heavy tasks. It also strengthens you emotionally and prevents future heart attacks. The hug of a dog reduces the level of your blood pressure, calms a tired mind, and forgives you of all your shortcomings that might be nagging you when you are all alone.

An exposure to certain bacteria associated with dogs will prevent asthma in the child. I learned this much later but I am certain that it did in Deepu. He was sickly and refused to eat the same plain rice with a pinch of salt for lunch every day. He refused to eat the small fishes that my father collected in his gamchha from the pond on Mondays. He refused to eat boiled eggs if we had some for the night. So there must have been breathlessness and exhaustion in him if it weren't for the little puppy's furry presence. He must have defended himself from all sorts of diseases due to the half year he spent with the puppy, he called Bhola.

Just as dogs bring home good health, it is also true that healthy homes can rear a dog without discomfort. On the foundation of fortune, if a dog is added, the health of the family doubles. You can buy all the luxuries for it and spend hours bathing it in a bath-tub. You can take it out for a walk in the mornings and evenings without concern for how to make ends meet during the day. You can walk for hours without exhaustion. You can play with fancy balls or sticks or an artificial chewing bone without planning for extra-time at work. In short, dogs bring health and health brings dogs home.

In our case, Deepu, the innocent one, brought home a dog without an inkling of how to provide for it.

*

One summer day, a farm-hand offered to sell ducklings in the nearby villages when they were a week old. There would be older ones too walking about behind their mothers. He offered to pick them up in a cane basket, enclosed on the top with a net, and carry them on his head. This opportunity on the farm came once or at the most three times in a year. The ducks waded in the pond and required little attention. The ducklings grew in number, enough to fill a basket and then the farm-hand negotiated with the owner to commission their sale.

One such man started early one morning at four. It took him three hours to reach our village. Many of us spotted him on the street and gathered around to try our luck with the rearing of ducklings. The privilege of eating a duck's egg was rare. It was a pure gamble. You could buy ten ducklings and expect half of them to survive and lay eggs. We sisters had a few coins and Deepu had some and we asked mother to contribute and then managed to buy four tiny ducklings. The smaller the birds, the lesser their life expectancy and therefore, they were cheaper. But we were a family of six people so we hoped to take care of them by taking turns. The main duty was to keep an eye on them. They were quite capable in the pond, wading all day, feeding on seeds, insects, and food grains from washed dishes and then walking back to the shelter of the home by themselves to sleep.

At first it was not easy to identify their gender. We believed the farm-hand who said that three of them were females. Two of them died in the next month, unable to survive the dirt that they consumed. The other two died next year. But before the fourth one died, she had delivered many eggs. Sometimes we had four, which could easily be consumed by the six of us, half each, sometimes there were only two, and then one day there would be six. For the most part only one duck was fertile.

*

On the stormiest nights, we had no sleep. We were constantly startled with the clatter of something flying off its due place. The red tiles of our roof were contributed by generous villagers. They were generous in the sense that it was a barter between tiles and some service rendered by mother or father. The tiles were neatly set by a mason whom we paid in cash. These clay tiles were a favourite discotheque for the monkeys.

Monkeys, old and young, monkeys with long and short tails, monkeys with infants clung to their breasts, monkeys with a white face, a black face or a tanned forehead, monkeys of all sizes and monkeys with all sizes of teeth came and danced on our roof.

The actual habitat of the monkeys was unknown to us. We wondered from where they would suddenly appear in the winters and clamour over our heads. Their squeaking roused the baby in the afternoon and my mother had difficulty putting him back to sleep. They would peep in through the window and also steal a little guava. They would rip off any clothes if my mother had the imprudence to leave drying on the clothesline outside. Their afternoon disco lasted for about half-an-hour and then suddenly, as if someone had called them from yonder, they'd rush off the roof and disappear into the wild.

The next day would be quite calm without the monkeys. The calm felt so soothing that we failed to notice the wind swishing on the tree-tops and the rush of a serpent near the puddle of mud accumulated from dripping leaves in the winter. In our area, serpents preferred the winters for showing up.

Now that the dance of the monkeys was over, winters gone, what we discover during a wild storm are cracks that would let in dripping water. The bamboos that held the tiles up would carry that seeping water to the end of the roof and save us the drops but in their turn begin to lose health. An unhealthy bamboo is a sure sign of unhealth for the family in near future.

The monsoons are relentless. No bamboo can save us from water dripping inside, right on top of our heads, where we might be lying at night. We need pots and buckets and mug and coconut shells to collect that water. We can't let the water flow inside the hut. We can't let the floor get muddy. That floor was all we had, to sit on, to lie on and to stand on and for the baby to crawl on. With water all over the floor, we can't call it a home, an indoors, a place for rest. We had to keep collecting the droplets in our utensils and throw them out from time to time. If the rains lasted for five hours at a stretch, my mother would appoint one sister at a time for this very task.

Health gave way to his alter-ego and erupted profusely in all parts of the body of my little brother every year while the monsoons lasted. He suffered from the allergy first when he was a toddler and was not going to school. Later on, when he joined school, he had to stay at home during the monsoons and the visible marks of his malaise was enough to explain why he missed school. When he was a teenager, he insisted on tolerating the pain and still went to school because there was something in the school that he liked very much.

*

The words diet and dieting are mutually opposite. Diet means eating and dieting means giving up eating. In common parlance if we ask, 'what is your daily diet' we mean what do you eat in a day, every day. But if we say, 'are you dieting', we mean are you skipping meals to avoid becoming obese.

In our household there was nothing to speak of diet. Our daily diet consisted of rice and salt, mostly, day in and day out. We could fetch a few potatoes in a week, trying to add taste to the rice with a mashed potato. Eggs were often donated by the grocer where my father worked. It was always a donation though a certain barter of labour was invariably involved. Call it over-time, which in offices fetch you a promotion in future. For my father, that extra labour, not really over-time, fetched some eggs for the growing children. You don't imagine he himself consumed such luxury. No. never. It was all for the children, neither mother nor father drooled over eggs. For them it was a forbidden luxury that would send them to hell after death.

With rice we also found some fish. Whatever little fish that could be caught in flowing water with my father's gamchha, it was fried in mustard oil and served to the children. I always received a couple of fish, whole, and ate it whole, head, belly and tail. It was crunchy and turned into a hard fibrous lump that was to be swallowed in one go.

Fish are nutritious. They keep the nerves going. They keep the skin intact and they also provide lubricant for the eyes and the brain and the nails. In a family, the daily consumption of a fish larger than half-a-kilo also promises muscles.

It was not difficult to get milk in those days. It has become more difficult now. I was born in 1973, Deepu in 1986 and now it is 2023. There has been a huge difference in the supply and distribution of milk. In those days milk was distributed by the milkman in its raw condition. My mother had to immediately boil it and give glassfuls to the children and prepare tea for herself and father and finish it altogether. Otherwise, the milk would require a second boiling which we did not wish to spend our fuel on. If left without boiling, the milk would spoil.

So, in a way, to sum up, milk, rice and fish was our daily diet. No fruits, no vegetables and no question of meat or chicken or nuts.

Dieting is just the opposite. It is a requirement when one no longer walks four kilometres on one's feet to join college or office. Dieting comes into the picture when one finds an abundance of fries and creamy things to eat. It's when you realise that such things were never required by your body, you start dieting.

We never needed dieting. We wanted diet.

*

Our other courses in food were dictated by the leftovers my sister brought home in those two precious years of her servitude in other households. Deepu was four years old at that time. It was easy for us sisters to assume that he brought poverty by birth. Soon enough, we also assumed that he brought sickness. My mother had a hard time believing that the so-called blessing from Ma Kali could be so pathetic. Still, we all toiled after him. We offered the best bites in the food that my sister brought home to him and took the rest for ourselves. He puked most of it and sometimes soiled his pants. Gradually, over the years, we learned to give him, not the tastiest, but the most basic food, like plain rice, boiled carrots or cooked dal. We consumed the nuts and bananas ourselves.

We were newly introduced to Indian breads. There would be many kinds of Indian breads, rotis, puris, parathas, kachoris and chops. Deepu got to eat only the rotis, that had no oil in them and we ate the rest of the breads. We also learned that at least in winters the puris and kachoris would last more than two days. What was left-over and wastes in those households on a special occasion, served as food for two or more days in our homes.

Nuts were a delicacy we savoured like people savour chocolates. Other than peanuts and chana roasts that vendors sold for a twenty five paisa coin, we received cashew-nuts and resins from wealthy villagers who wished to distribute something to children on puja days. We ate handfuls of those nuts and often regretted it. Our stomachs were simply not accustomed to heavy food.

It may be believed that different foods are designed for different people. The poor can easily digest raw milk or stale rotis while the rich can digest nuts and berries easily. Human beings would prefer to believe that the stomachs are designed according to the family one is born in, but the truth is, the stomach gets accustomed to a certain diet over time and this explains why, after earning riches, many poor people continue to enjoy the old diet and fall sick if new food items are introduced to them, even when those are affordable.

Our diet, though, changed for better varieties for those two long years when my father had nothing to do except cleaning up a part of the untended fruit orchard in the vain hope of getting a bunch of bananas or some mangoes, our health deteriorated in many ways.

*

Health and fitness go together as the most desirable thing in the world. One of the easiest ways of losing fitness is overwork. Another quiet killer is worry.

Worries appeared when any of our chappals got torn. Our habit was to buy leather chappals from the shop and then take them straight to the cobbler to reinforce the stitches. These leather chappals lasted a lifetime. It was devastating if one such strong chappal got torn by some accident.

Our first prayer would be to the cobbler to mend it somehow. But a torn piece of leather could not be mended. Usually, rubber pieces were available for repair work. If the sole of a chappal wore out, the cobbler offered a layer of rubber underneath. Leather was not available as loose pieces.

Worries appeared when an unfortunate incident dented a wheel of one's bicycle. We never had a bicycle to own but we often borrowed one from the grocer. It was when we had a special errand and did not need to board a bus or train for that purpose. We took the bicycle, went to the location, and returned in an hour. For this, the grocer never asked for anything in exchange. It was our duty to see that the tyres were full and the gear was not creaking. It was for our good that we took the bicycle to the cycle repair shop first and got it greased and the tyres filled with air before starting off on our journey. That was all it entailed.

But once my sister did fall from a bicycle and went crashing against a horse-cart on the road. The horse looked frightened by the little girl in a black frock and snorted and took a few steps backwards and one of his hooves landed on the spokes of the bicycle that was sprawled beneath him. There occurred a dent.

The spoke had to be replaced at our cost. We did not have enough money to spare and the grocer reminded us of the cost for a couple of days. My mother worried a lot. She lost much of her vitality due to worries after Deepu was born and I was foremost in believing and whispering it to my sisters that he was a natural curse on the family.

Worries were endless. Even when my younger sister was relieved of the services in other homes, there was tremendous worry about the wedding ceremony. I was capable of doing most of the running about and kept worries at bay. My mother spent time at home worrying. Her anxieties were mostly built on imaginary things. She had an abject fear of relatives, especially the siblings of the groom and however repeatedly we assured her that there were no one of the kind in the groom's family, that all his elder sisters were married off and well settled, she worried that there might erupt someone late in life or someone who was lost and would be found later. She worried if any of the parents had any secret ailments that would require her daughter to attend to throughout her life. Such fears were not altogether baseless, as she had herself suffered a lot in the hands of my father's siblings.

In everything that we arranged for my sister, a constant fear of her losing those things dictated our choice. If it was a mere anklet, a silver anklet that I bought, I warned her a hundred times that she should not take it off her ankles. I meant that she should not gift it to anyone who asks for it but I could never bring myself to say that because that was like asking for the impossible. All I hoped was that people would be so disgusted with the thing around her ugly feet that no one would want it for themselves. About necklaces, there was no such security. Someone would certainly ask for it and she would have to give it away without a grimace. That's how I looked at the anklets as the only pieces of ornament that she could hang on to.

Thankfully, these were only dreads and she was lucky enough to have no such people to take away her rightful belongings. Not everybody gets a home like she got.

*

There were many guava trees. Guavas tend to attract birds and insects. If a guava tree is infested with red ants its fruits don't last to ripen. The ants eat unripe guavas also. If any fruit is penetrated by a worm, it ripens suddenly and drops to the ground. If by chance a tree has been spared by the ants, the fruit ripens into light green colour and all the parrots peck at them. Those half-eaten guavas drop to the ground and it smells heavenly. Guavas smell like any fragrant flower. I love its smell. But as long as it doesn't smell, it is worth eating. My father had cleared the climbers from guava trees but he had not managed to get rid of the insects. It was because the tree is very strong and can let the insects ravish it as much as they liked, until in the winter season, it recovered its strength again.

Still, many times in December, we got a few guavas from some of the good trees. There would be a cluster of three fruits out of which the middle one would remain unreachable to the birds. It grew healthy for us to consume.

There were so many mango trees but not one was left to ripen. The storms blew away most of the blooms and if there were fruits, the next storm dropped them to the ground, still green. We liked those green mangoes but too much of them can upset the stomach. We used to collect some and take them to the school to distribute them to our friends.

Bananas are nutritious and a fruit easily grown in wet coastal lands. In our lands, near the foothills, banana trees often do not bear the edible yellow fruits. In its place we get green bananas that would never ripen and we call them unripe bananas. It is just another breed of green bananas that taste bitter and remain more fibrous. These are iron rich vegetables that people cook with potatoes and bitter gourd, bottle gourd and tomatoes. They can also be consumed with rice after boiling with salt. My father fetched such unripe bananas from the fruit orchard around us. He also found the womb of the banana trees, called mocha and that too can be easily cut to pieces and boiled.

We loved those rainy days when there would be a large mocha to eat. It was rather sad for my father because he brought home the mocha of a pregnant banana tree that the storm had brought down to the ground. It was a great loss for the future but for the present, a great feast in our house.

Banana trees grow out in small saplings around the fallen ones. The next year, there would be a new pregnant tree, he knew it, but he was always saddened. It also meant, no green bananas. We simply did not care what he thought until one day, Deepu penetrated his heart with fervent questions. It was Deepu who brought out the sentiments in him and then there was no stopping his tirade about fortune, its connection to health and its connection to education.

*

Deepu started going to school at the age of six. By then my immediate sister had finished school and was training as a tailor. She did not continue her education on account of me. She saw me going kilometres on foot and then returning home fully exhausted and it just settled in her mind that college work was not meant for her. She preferred working in a sitting position and tailoring was a good idea. She found a tailor in the village who needed an apprentice and willingly took her in. He was a familiar face in the village and his place was not far away from our hut. My father approved of her choice and gave her his blessings.

Deepu became my father's next concern. It was just the beginning of his career and he had a long way to traverse before reaching the stage of his elder sisters. He came late, he would take time and now, in 2023, we know that he continued and continued to study.

I believe that my father's understanding of the situation of the pregnant banana tree, that blended fortune with health and education, made a huge difference to Deepu's outlook on life. The inspiration lasted for countless years and even though he may not be able to trace the connection himself, we sisters know it for sure that my father made a huge impression on him when he was supposed to relish the mocha, and when instead, he found his father morose and inquired of the reason and then found a valid explanation and it went into his head like an ignited lamp, the thought of education somehow buried deep into his guts where the mocha refused to find place.

We bought him new chappals. For his smaller feet, there was a possibility of buying rubber sandals. It was in the year 1992, he was barely six but the school admitted him in July and he was tremendously happy. He had trotted to our school compound earlier as a kid holding his father's hand and anticipated the day he would be a member of it. Now, he entered the compound holding his slate and chalk in one hand and his little tiffin wrapped in Sal leaves in the other.

He was not accustomed to wearing chappals. He often took them off in school. We saw his dirty footprints on the chappals and scolded him a lot. Dirt on the upper sole of the chappals ruined it sooner than we could afford. He understood that and soon we discovered that he washed his feet before wearing the chappals back after the bell rang. We had to warn him again that the wet feet ruined the leather. This went on until one day he asked for rubber sandals.

Fortune plus health plus education was forming a circle round my head at dawn one winter. I learned it the hard way that these were all connected. He learned it intuitively. The more I went to teach the lepers, the more I resented the lack of fortune. I saw no merit in education, so far and I was angry with Deepu for ruining his first pair of chappals. He understood intuitively that we were missing the point. We were asking him to learn from tradition whereas, he wanted to learn it scientifically. He was certain that the solution lay in wearing rubber sandals and sparing the leather altogether.

Children of his age went to school without food. Many children did not even get milk. In our village the condition was better but in other villages, the situation was very bad. Little girls in oversized frocks would vomit first thing in the morning and dirty themselves and teachers would clean them and even wash the frocks. All day, they would be roaming about happily in their bloomers. School is nothing more than a playpen. The alphabet they learn is a simple task. For the rest of the day, there is storytelling and games, clay modelling and drawing that brings them joy. Nobody likes to leave school, their friends, and the large playground. In the afternoon, once the frocks have dried in the sun, they are made to wear them again and pick up their slates and walk back home in a group.

Mid-day meals are distributed now and many children come to the school only for the meal. Their parents see the advantage only in terms of food. Teachers see the advantage in education. The meal attracts the kids like flies and then teachers trap them into discipline and learning. After a couple of years in the school, where rooms are fewer than the number of classes required according to the age groups, many kids try to evade the classroom and play outside until the food is served.

It is the teachers who bring discipline into their lives. It is a tough call. To make the children come to the school, meals work well, but keeping them still and paying attention to the lessons on the blackboard is another challenge. Once away from the parents, teachers act as pseudo-parent and somehow it is accepted by one and all that these people will do no harm to the little ones.

Health is of paramount importance. Here, in the school, there is no dearth of donations from the outside world. Wherever there is poverty, the camera lens focuses on it and through those lenses, the world gets to see them and pour out their sympathies in kind. Clothes, water bottles, bags, ask for anything, it's there for distribution. That such things go to the rightful needy is determined by the ones who draw the lenses in our direction. Rarely does such kindness go unfulfilled.

Deepu understood the nature of difficulties associated with primary school from his very first day. He was horrified to see someone fainting after a bout of dysentery. He was struck by the sight of unsteady hands trying to draw a hut. He was overwhelmed by the amount of shouting and repeating the teacher had to do to bring about a little positive response from little girls.

He saw confused frightened eyes, dazed sleepy eyes, unkempt flying hair, infested with lice, torn hems of frocks and many boys in oversized shorts. He saw rickety legs and disfigured toes due to injury, and many deformities of the body that came out from the mother's malnourished womb.

After joining school, Deepu's complaints about food and mosquitoes vanished. He found a new mission, that of carrying tit-bits of fruits or an extra potato in his tiffin box for his friends. He saved his chalks for a friend, brushed his friends' hair with his own comb that he carried for the purpose, concealed from his mother. He took the precious nail-cutter to the school and clipped the fingernails of many girls and boys.

He spoke softly, persuasively, and unstoppably. The teachers silently observed his kindness and did not confiscate the comb or the nail-cutter. We were the ones who got angry with him for squandering our hard-earned belongings on his friends. And we said, obviously, the teachers would be happy that he was doing their job.

Health attracts health, wealth attracts wealth, weakness attracts weakness, happiness attracts happiness. It was plain in view in the school. Children grouped together according to their propensities. Deepu had a host of friends, primarily the ones who learned the alphabet fast and spent the rest of their time at school, studying their classmates.

*

One evening Deepu returned home with a thorn pierced in his right big toe. He was limping and tears ran down his cheeks. He was grown up and wise enough by now not to howl like an imbecile. He just clenched his fists and limped all the way home. The thorn was thin but long. We managed to extract it and bandaged the wound. We had cotton strips and mercurochrome at home. The next day my father bought a tablet of pain-killer for him. That was all.

He did not go to school that day. He ran a fever in the night and by the next morning, his toe had swollen up. We applied some warm water to his toe and a cold patch on his forehead. The day went by in suspense. We did not take him to the hospital although it had crossed my mind that he should be saved from tetanus.

Those vaccines of tetanus and BCG and polio had reached our district. I knew that Deepu had been safe from many diseases. But still, the fever was worrying.

By night the swelling and the fever subsided and we thought that the worst was over. The next day he insisted on going to school and we took it as a sign of complete recovery.

A few days later, it was a Sunday and Deepu was lying on the mat with his right leg poised over the left. I could see the sole of his foot. It seemed to have become very white. I went closer to have a look at the wound and sure enough, there was a big corn. The skin had tightened in defence around the piece of thorn, a foreign body by definition, and formed a large lump of dead flesh. Now the body had rejected that part and would not even try to spew out the foreign body. It would remain like the ghost of a toe for the rest of his life, I guessed.

The thorn was long and it had broken inside his flesh. We thought that it had been extracted but actually a broken piece was still inside. The flesh was enclosed around it.

I had a word with my father about it. He agreed that the corn should be treated. Deepu had switched it out of his mind and walked with the big toe raised from the ground. It changed his gait slightly but we had not noticed it. Now that I was sure about the corn, I accosted him with questions such as, how much does it hurt.

Deepu had neglected the growth of such a deformity in his body. He had considered the thorny affair, over and done with. He did not wish to spend time on it particularly because that would make him miss school.

As my father had said, fortune and health and education formed a complete circle. One without the other was an incomplete ladder on the way to heaven. For lack of fortune, lack of nutrition and lack of understanding, one came crashing down in the middle of the storm like that giant banana tree.

He was not at all happy to go to the hospital. He ran away to school early in the morning. We had work so we forgot about it for a week until Sunday, when we were together at home and he lay on the mat with the corn raised up, precisely because it hurt.

The next week went by without a visit to the hospital. Soon we failed to notice the corn. It had become a hard nut and he alone knew how unhealthy it was. For the body has that alter-ego of health called allergy and the corn is that kind of skin allergy that prevents the spread of infection to its other parts. It keeps the body going and the deformity is more or less a part of nature. We can see hundreds of deformed animals roaming the planet and probably, except for mankind, no one cares to find a cure.

But the human mind revolts against living like animals. All medical science is a revolt against nature. All the methods of cure are for one ailing body, one individual that is part of the group and the health of the group depends on the cure for each individual's ailment. So, Deepu's corn drew our attention on Sundays. Each Sunday we wanted a cure and every Monday we went on with our work, neglecting our heart.

He must have borne the corn for about two years until we had to buy him a new pair of chappals. That was when he brought up the subject again and insisted on rubber sandals. We bought him rubber sandals and immediately took him to the hospital. The doctor examined his corn and suggested a remedy.

It must be removed by surgery.

CHAPTER THREE: FAMILY

ORPHANS HAVE NO family. Unless they are brought-up in a home, they are destitute who would not survive even a year. The same is with all living creatures. Over the centuries, human families have grown a system. The system defines who is family and who is a neighbour. There is a cousin of family and that's called relatives. Unfortunately, relatives tend to stand apart and create havoc in one's life. That's how we distinguish family from relative and choose whom to send out of the periphery of our day-to-day existence.

My mother had an abject fear of relatives. After my younger sister was married off, she often whimpered in her sleep. I could hear her mumble distinct words in the night. She recalled all her trauma during her stay with relatives on my father's side. Although for him, once they were family, for my mother, as sisters and brothers in law, they were a menace and for us, therefore, not uncle or aunt but 'relatives'. We chose to keep a polite distance from them, physically apart in a different village and mentally struck off as non-existent.

My father suffered no qualms about this arrangement. He knew it all as the past and his present involved his children. Being the eldest among his siblings he had offered his wealth, his services and his time in bringing them up to adulthood. After that, if he took to his heels with his wife and babies, it was instinctive. He had to do it to meet the basic need for survival. He had found work as gatekeeper of his uncle's bungalow and that was a good excuse for his departure.

For my mother, it was a great relief. Until the time that she had to send off her own daughter to a stranger's home, she had forgotten the past, like all trauma is shoved to the darkest recesses of the mind as a nightmare. It reemerged from those recesses in her sleep and disturbed me. I could not stop myself from asking her about those noises that she made in the night and I was horrified to know of the atrocity relatives can hurl on you.

Being a woman, I was filled with chagrin. Being a daughter, I felt vengeful. Being a family, I pitied my mother.

Trauma, hunger and hard work tears down a body, but not the will. Through decades, my mother has toiled hard to keep us happy. She barely lost her patience and more often than not, provided for us, whatever was possible. But this back story of her life after marriage was unknown to us children. It's from the time when she was carrying me in her womb.

It sounds like a warm, comfortable place, the womb. But nourishment of the womb is a difficult task. Even wealthy people fail to cater to the needs of the womb in an adequate manner. Some eat too much fat, some eat heavy dal, some eat only fruits, some ask for pickles, some for jams, some parents force nuts down your throat that you ultimately throw up. Carrying a baby is always a health hazard. For all those precious months, you have to watch your walk, your burden and your clothing. If you have an appetite, you have to resist the spicy things and if the weather changes, you have to prevent fever.

Everything is overlooked by the ugly cousin called relatives. They would visit you at the wrong time. They would express strong sentiments if you fail to answer their invitations. They would sit surrounding your extended tummy and meanly express their conjectures about baby boy or girl. They would give you a headache.

None of these might be traumatic. You can even take it all with a smile. You can love your relatives for giving a thought to your condition. But what if you had a relative who snatched the bowl of rice from your hands when you were hungry?

So, if my mother suffers from nightmares about the in-laws of my sister, she is not dreaming. She is reliving that moment when her sister-in-law rushed into the kitchen and snatched the bowl of boiled rice from her hands and upturned it on her head. The rice with its wet starch streamed down her head and shoulders and soon she had red blisters all over. Her head was scalded and the sister-in-law darted out of the kitchen shrieking obscenities.

I was in her womb then. Four months old. There were another five months to go. It is thanks to the neighbours that I have turned out healthy, better even than Deepu. My grandfather was confined to his room with that horrible tuberculosis, my father was out-of-doors working as an attendant in a shop, my mother was helpless. Being the housewife, wedded to an enormous family of four sisters and three brothers was slavery. Those relatives did not work at all. They were big burdens. If they went to school, it was a blessing that they would one day provide for themselves, but that was a long way off. In the present, for my mother, it was slaving to feed and clean up for nine members, including herself.

The early morning chores started at four when it was still dark. She would take two buckets to the pond to fill and carry back home. There she also bathed and washed the clothes all by herself. When she returned with the buckets, she left with a pot to bring water from the well. It was further away and the water was chilling and fresh. It was shallow water and many particles of plants floated in it. Back home, her job was to filter it using a gamchha.

She used that water to cook food. While cooking, it was normal for her to feel hungry. The aroma of boiled rice was always appetising. But she desisted. She served food to every member of the family, particularly to those who would leave early and then sat down to eat. By then the food would be cold and meagre.

That fateful day, unable to control her hunger, she had poured herself some rice along with the boiling starch from the cooking pot. It was that hot mass that her sister-in-law upturned on her head.

Though mother rushed to the bucket and splashed water to assuage the burns, the blisters showed up and everybody got to see the damage.

For the following months, the neighbours must have given her more food than she found at home. In that sense, I am the product of the whole community. I belong to that community, which took pity on my pregnant mother and offered their leftovers to her. It was obvious that father did not do much to tackle his siblings. He was always jeered at for being the karta, the eldest son with hundreds of responsibilities and not a single grateful soul around.

Both of them bore their responsibilities, but when enough was enough, they left the place. All of my mother's jewellery, her sarees and whatever uncle gifted her from time to time, went to the sisters, or were sold off for their education. One brother did finish his schooling and managed to raise a grocery business, but that was all. He never looked back to repay his elder brother. He has never cuddled us or sent us any gifts.

That's why relatives are non-existent for us.

*

Uncle is no more. This is the sad truth of life, all the good souls depart for heaven sooner than the sinners. Uncle left us when he was seventy. He was family. He loved us. We spent lovely days in his house. We loved him. But then, cousins came into the scene and they were jealous creatures.

Oscillating between love and dislike, we visited our uncle when school was closed for the summers. But that was all. The cousins hardly visited us. We forgot their good names, the interaction was only superficial, restricted to the indoors of uncle's house. How they fared in later life, hardly affected us.

One nephew, in particular, has actually grown into an officer in the colliery. He is well off and would have definitely found me or my sister a good position. But he hardly knew us. He saw us off at the railway station when we were children and I am pretty sure, he has mixed up our names by now.

Poor relatives are suckers. That's the old adage and however tied to the roots each one of us may be by the common surname, or gotra or ancestor or rishi or community, each individual evaluates the other in terms of their wealth. If you live in a one thousand square feet of land gifted to you by a distant grandfather, others will skirt around you for fear of your asking for more donations.

We haven't grown so rich that our wealth might attract relatives. We have simply stood up on our feet. We have no bigger a house than that one thousand square feet. The benevolent grandfather is no more and his children are strangers to us. People seek familiarity only if you grow bigger than them in worth. Those days might eventually show up, might show up in the lives of our children, as I said, fortune is fickle. She travels from one home to another after a spell.

Memories of interaction with relatives should be shoved to the dark recesses of our mind. Otherwise, they can interfere with the everyday judgment of our fellow beings. When mother recalled the dread of being ill-treated by her sister-in-law, a slip of a girl, two years younger than her, but authoritative in the household, she poured out many stories of injustice.

One such story was of the travail of collecting water from the well. Only very few people owned a rope to hang down into the well. If you went there with a vessel but no rope, you must borrow one. It was a bargain. The owner of the rope was wealthy and his wealth shown in the number of buckets he owned. He would fill up twenty of his buckets with the help of that rope. His formula was, I'll lend you the rope and you lend me your labour.

No one was irrationally generous. During the pandemic, we noticed how irrationally, Mother Nature was generous, and how equally irrational was her fury. The Amphan shook us all right in the midst of a viral infection that was water borne. Her generosity shown in the way she recovered her ozone layer and in the way all the rivers were restored to their ancient purity within fifteen days of the Lockdown. We admired her generosity and for once we realised that in nature there was plenty even during adversity. In Mother Nature, the beauty lay in doing only the necessary things. She always replenished herself in a sort of irrational cycle. Whereas, humans work on the principle of rationality.

Humans are never irrationally generous. If there is one such being, he is viewed by all others as a curio. I was beginning to see such a curio in Deepu.

Our relatives had bargained the privileges out of our hands. The house belonged to their father but the cleaning and maintenance fell upon my mother's shoulders. She had brought with her a lot of gold jewellery, but decisions regarding their use went to the relatives. It was impossible for me to see it as logically right. I was driven to tears when my mother narrated the incident when I was barely five years old and my grandfather, the tuberculosis ridden thin frame that hardly left the bed, deposited all his phlegm onto the bedside floor. The disease ridden mucus with blobs of blood and a smearing of the morning tea formed a distressing sight and stench. My mother had been to the well and was taking a long time to return. The other inmates of the house, grandfather's own offspring, felt no compulsion to clean it up. They grew impatient as they waited for my mother to return and finally, with gross callousness, directed me to clean up the mess.

I had no idea how to go about it. My mother told me that when she returned home, I had soiled not only my little hands in an attempt to pick up the slime, but I had also frequently touched my hair and frock with them and thereby triggered a fear of contracting the communicable disease.

Mother had, of course, picked me up and done the rest of the cleaning herself, something she was accustomed to do as irrationally as she was accustomed to cook food for that bunch of relatives. It did not matter to those fools that she was the same person doing the morning pooja and the emptying of the garbage. All duty lay upon the karta and his spouse. This irrational system that made the bungalow unlivable, actually wronged my parents further because traditionally, the eldest son, as karta, was supposed to inherit it and all the other siblings were subordinated to him. In many families, only the karta remains in the inherited house and the younger siblings move out and fend for themselves.

Not with the kind of ill-luck my mother was married to. My father's gentle nature was exploited and like Mother Earth, he too bore it and later, replenished himself in the form of his brilliant offspring. The circle of fortune, health, and education, though ruptured for a while by the twin accidents of my grandfathers on either side, recovered its shape in our generation.

The little five-year-old was rubbed and scrubbed with ample soap and given a fresh frock to wear and was spared the contagion. That little me, I can visualise now, must have hated the cold water, the dowsing and lathering more than the slime which she was not particularly warned about. Little children do not mind smells, unless some chemical strikes their nostrils painfully. Kids play in the muck, grab slimy insects, sit in a pool of urine, scatter a mix of food with soil and some kids love using clay as body-scrub with tremendous satisfaction. That clayey substance might sometimes be discovered to be the same body's excreta also.

So, I pity mother more than that five-year-old who suffered no trauma as such. She was just an instance of the cruelty relatives can do.

*

Relatives do worse, as Deepu told me about the ignorant Muslim community where little girls are married off as barter for feeding the boys at home. It is not that they have an easy life at the cost of females. But the temporary relief is irrational. It is a lack of foresight that makes those families give away an eleven-year-old to a man for sex.

The boys are fed to be butchered in the grime of construction sites. Many fourteen-year-olds, once they begin to look tall and masculine, go out with their fathers or uncles to toil in the strange cities far away from their mothers. They get dirty food, meagre shelter and all sorts of bad company, learning to suck at beedi, paan and fermented food that works as an intoxicant. They are certain school drop-outs who never reach the rung of education, and therefore the circle of fortune, health, and education is never complete for them. It is the same quagmire of family and relatives that they wallow in generation after generation.

There is no escape. The injunction to eat, drink and procreate seems to have dawned upon them from heaven. They are earthlings and still they do not see the system of the earth. Mother Nature never nurtures a weakling. Mother Nature throws out the infirm and the dwindling kind. She wants to be watered by the wealth of the worthy people. She strikes down the poor, the illiterate, and the burdens on her soil, by leaving them grovelling on the pathway. That's the scene we encountered during the pandemic. They could not be saved because they were too many and too worthless. They went under in great numbers and it was not possible to count them, by name and family and village. They just went under en masse. The enormity of their deaths was only visible in the graveyard and the cremation grounds. Those whose circle of fortune-health-education was simply too torn, too rundown, too faint or too exhausted, all succumbed to the mass slaughter of irrational Mother Nature.

The lesson thereof? Keep your number small. Take care of everyone as an individual. Take nourishment, wealth and learning seriously. Be angry when the child refuses to go to school. Be prepared to pay the fees. Be ready with her tiffin in the morning. It is that simple. One or two years of drought, disease or danger of any kind should not be your doom. You should be able to count your family on your finger tips and be able to save each and everyone from the deluge.

Yet, it was evident from the sight of a man wheeling a little girl on his bicycle that she has been bought flesh and blood and soul and brain, altogether to be ravaged and her entrails be torn to produce a mass of similar such creatures who can't defend themselves from the fury of Mother Nature.

The beatings and humiliations a girl suffered from her parents when she refused to get married, further showed us how insane the system was. Deepu ventured to save a few hearts from bleeding at the altar of marriage, but he too was left helpless amid the scavenging relatives.

*

The role of a reformer, then, is not pleasant. If I were to become a political leader, I would abstain from the role of a reformer. It's because I thrive on votes from the very nasty people who need reforming. Even if I knew that the overthrow of the deep-rooted system that has erupted on the surface of our land like a weed, is for general good, I would refrain from doing it myself. A political leader, by definition, is not a reformist. He is the passenger at the back seat that can give commands and let the driver risk the navigation.

The role of a reformer is risky. Anybody, any day, might take offence to the level of wringing your neck. You may have all sorts of arguments, scientific, moral, scriptural, anything as evidence of your good intention, but for a villager, impoverished in health, brain and body, would never understand you. He doesn't have any vision. He lives from hand to mouth and can only see as far as the grub in his hand, a reformer might bribe a man to obey him unconditionally, but there is hardly any enlightening from the inside. Therefore, after a while, the reformer is sacrificed and the only thing the passenger at the back seat does is to change the driver.

If I were to talk to the lepers about medicine, the appeal would fall flat. I could not reason with them who were starving. When they saw kindness in the eyes of commuters at the railway station, they forgot all about health and preferred the puri that they would get immediately with the coin dropped charitably by a commuter in their crippled hands. The puri is more vital than the medicines. The crippled hands become their bread-earners and they don't need a future to it.

They have no vision of a better future and they lack the possibility of nearing that kind of life because it's a big family, lots of relatives who are plaguing each other and each evening closes with the intoxication of fermented rice.

To try to think, the brain cells have to be exercised from very early on. Cognition increases with better health. There was a time when food was not part of the school's course. It was introduced by the hard effort of a reformist, someone who took the driver's seat and was backed by politicians in the long run. They saw in him the substance of progress in the society and they did not want to pose an opposition to the regressive norms, so they stayed away from direct confrontation with the public. They visited like guests, appreciated the efforts of the reformer and slid into the back seat and watched from a distance. They became the real heroes at the time of elections.

Imagine a ten-year-old being benefited by the mid-day meal and later, at twenty, he has to vote for a particular leader. Would he choose the lanky reformer from those ten years ago, who looked like begging before his father to send him to school and who served him a spoonful of dal at lunch? No. He would look up to the burly politician who had visited the school, garlanded and seated with dignity, lecturing on the benefits of nutrition and patting the back of the reformer with his enormous hands. In his rational head, he would conceive that nothing would have been possible without the backing nod of the politician and power belonged to him.

Imagine his father, grey bearded and contentedly licking his fingers after a sumptuous meal, reflecting on the change of fortune. Would he thank the reformer for that unpleasant scuffle that made him send the grown-up boy to school? He would still feel that if the reformer had not intervened, money would have flown in from that very day when the boy was made to drop out of school and go to work at a construction site. The power of the reformer is in his navigation skills while the power of success lay in the passenger seat that hides the owner of the vehicle.

To stop one child marriage in a gang of sixty interlinked family members in a Muslim community where the bride and groom might just be living in the neighbouring houses, a reformer might encounter death threats. No politician goes to such places. Yet, it pains me to think, Deepu nurtured that kind of tendency.

Were I to restrain him, he would have curled up in his shell and exploded one day. And who was I to restrain him, anyway? I had the fear of the lepers, I applied for a transfer and then failed. I toiled in those areas for a couple of years and then looked for another job. I could not act as a reformer and value their lives over my own. And what kind of sacrifice is that? Keeping the sacrifices of my parents in bringing us up as educated and capable, I had no heart to lavish that hard-earned better life to the profanities and profligacy of that irrational tribe. I got away.

*

Marriage, I realised gradually, is not the only curse of womanhood. Women do get into marriages that compromise their dignity. Their health is compromised further in child-bearing. But the worst scenario I came across is when there is a divorce. Again, in the Muslim community, this is more apparent. Divorced women come back to their parents. They feel free to wander out again. Many of them remarry. But if someone's heart has been roughed up in the first marriage, she desists more such encounters. The parents know at one point of time that the woman is of no more use to the community but as a flesh to be sold.

We don't do it openly. A secret is something that is whispered to every ear. That's how we know it all and yet don't know it at all. We can never be sure where they go, how they spend their days in the cities for the better part of winter, and how they come back hale and hearty, loaded with gifts of scrunchies and frilly frocks and sandals and chocolates for their little nieces and nephews. It seems irrational. Yet, it works rationally well for the family. No harm done and if there's an internal damage, of the heart, the soul, the guts or the uterus, it was too internal to be debated by family members. The face glowed, the skin shone and the flesh curved.

Summers diminished the health of the flesh and the skin and the face all over again. On the contrary, it was summers when the men in the family ventured out with a self-appointed leader, who gathered them up like a club manager and arranged for their departure to foreign lands. The women did not get to go to those exotic places. Kerala, God's own Land, Chandigarh, the City Beautiful, Delhi, the Capital of the Nation, to speak of a few familiar names that the boys uttered. It must be gorgeous locations that attracted them in hordes, and then one fine morning at the beginning of winter sent them back home to rest in starvation. The money they sent or saved and brought home did not last the whole of winters, feeding, repairs, medicines, and school. All of them starved, one time or the other. Mortality brought them to the conclusion that there should be more and many more children. The ugly nexus of poverty-sickness-ignorance never left them at all.

You can't always blame Mother Nature for lashing out at them after this.

*

The blood and sweat that we lose in the horrible job at the furnace is incomprehensible for a Babu. I live in Babu Para, meaning the affluent white collared gentleman's colony, albeit at the furthest end of the lane, in the smallest house, and greet all others with the humblest of gestures. But still, being an upper caste, teaching class, and descendants of zamindars, I escaped that furnace-like existence. My parents ensured the education of their children and once my sister and once my brother did top the class in school. So, I did not happen to lose my blood and sweat in the way those backward classes did.

As teachers, at the primary level, the task is very tough. You are expected to eradicate that specific type of backwardness. We were poor, lacked money, but our intellect was superior. Those classes of people, that my litany is drawing, lack that intellect, by blood.

Their longevity is affected by their toil. Those furnaces they work at for up to four hours in a day, standing under the relentless sun, at proximity of around one thousand degrees of temperature, and the liquid metal pouring out of its bowels, wearing a wet jute-sack, nothing of the person remains except a walking carcass. No thought, no emotion, no feeling can surface in such severe conditions. Fatigue and hunger overtake you the moment you step down, replaced by another poor mortal taking your place as the sacrificial human in the human-made world.

To bring reason and vision in their minds is like digging the barren bedrocks of the ocean. There's plenty on the surface but nothing is absorbed by these minds. They are dry, hard nuts that live like discarded foliage in the jungle of the human race. Taking pity on them and acting as a reformer is like turning into a scapegoat, on whom all the blame would be flung at the end of the day.

If the downtrodden have been mobilised in any way towards progress, it is through the idea that they need extra charity. Charity has become their birthright. I was brought up poor but I lived with a great sense of dignity, that someday, I shall not have to expect charity from others. We have done even better than that. We have ourselves turned charitable.

But hard labour for generations, poor cognition under dire physical stress, low nutrition, lack of dreams, and the added effect of intoxicants have driven these clusters of poor folk to expect nothing by themselves but charity from others.

A school in their village is many things more than a place for learning the alphabet. A child is a tug of war between parent and teacher. There is no school fee, the only thing required is time. But the child is still not sent to school. The older generation of teachers has tired of taking attendance. If someone is missing, she's missing, that's all. How long can one run after missing children when there are forty others who need to be attended to while they are at school?

All of them are in primary school. The school building in this village is small. There are two rooms to accommodate the village children of all ages up to ten. After primary level, the child is supposed to go to the school beyond the village, walk another kilometre and study hard. Here, only six- to ten-year-olds huddled together to get education in basic reading, writing, and arithmetic, environment science and general knowledge. It is the teachers who study hard.

Higher education, that after school level, is coveted. You go to college because you want to study. But primary education is forced. Primary education is like bitter medicine. For most children, it does not suit the palate. Teachers must force it down their throats. Some tactics are required. In modern times, the science of education includes psychology. You have to observe the child and find a way of teaching that does not cause her distress.

Earlier, pathshalas were run on the concept of aptitude for learning. Not every child was expected to take to the alphabet. If not interested, there were hundreds of professions that did not require reading and writing. On job training started at age six and it was mostly the father's profession that was adopted by every child. You got very few children to teach, those who were intrigued by the letters and who had an innate liking for deeper knowledge, such as an interest in the workings of the cosmos or a desire to know why tree leaves turned brown in winter.

Now, learning has been recognized as a source of uplifting the whole community. It is not the family that decides if a child should go to school. The government injunction is to send every child to school, not allow child labour and not ignore a school drop-out. And to this purpose, the training of a primary level teacher includes child psychology.

But the task is tougher when you must understand the parents' psychology also. You must counter the changes in physiognomy at puberty. You must learn communication skills, read wordless expressions, and read the entire psychology of the village just like a participant sociologist. It is a complex task and Deepu set his foot into that circle, quite involuntarily at first when he found employment.

*

If a skill runs in the family, the children learn it quickly. If it is carpentry, the children learn to hew and chisel without a thought. If the same skill is taught to a bunch of students in a primary school, the course would end in wastage of wood and also some chopped fingers.

If a parent makes his child his apprentice, the tutoring goes on day and night. The child gets to watch him all the time doing the same kind of work. A garage mechanic would be giving a running commentary on his actions while his children are around and even give them harmless trials on an endless number of broken down cars. If the wiring of the car engine is taught in schools, there would be one demo of one model in perfect condition and the wiring and rewiring would pose no great mental pressure on the pupils to learn the steps.

At some point of time, learning the alphabet in school became more important than learning how to repair a car. Even if the books were teaching about motor-vehicles, it was the use of the words, for reading and reproduction in the exams, that became more important than the use of the pliers and screws.

And we do believe that schools provide knowledge of distant things, like the solar system, that would be useful in our future, say, for becoming philosophical about our status in the universe and perhaps recognizing the fruitlessness of the sacrifice of a life.

And one day, if this philosophy, above everything else, appeals to us as an explanation for not working, not giving importance to the requirements of a bed, a bicycle and winter clothing, the family is doomed.

Moral lessons are intrinsically built to contradict the dictates of the guts. We are morally right if we give up our bread for someone else, said Tolstoy. We are morally right if we own up a lie, accept punishment for it, said Swami Vivekananda. We are morally right if we tug water out of a well for people we do not know and then get late for one's home, said Dr. Radhakrishnan. We are morally right when we do not counterattack when an oppressor hits us, said Bapu.

Back home, bleeding, if you collapse in your mother's arms, your morals are turned upside down. The little piece of bread that she had packed for your lunch was her investment towards a secure future in your arms. That lie which would have saved your attendance in class, erupted into further cause for lies, told to your mother. That water which you were to fetch for your mother, got delayed and in some cases, missed altogether. If you had no such moral lessons to assimilate in your life, you were better off. You were more inclined to rely on your gut feeling. Because, by birth, the dictates of the guts are good for the family.

A reformer, therefore, went beyond the dictates of his guts.

*

A family is the centre of happiness. So, when the puppy named Bhola gave us happiness, he became a member of our family. Because of his peculiar habits, he was given an ante-room. The roof of this room was built with straw, not tiles but the mud walls sheltered him from the wind and the sun very well. In the rainy season, he often whimpered and Deepu went out to check if the straw roof was leaking. He had tucked some loose sheets of plastic into the straw for him.

A family also shares a common unhappiness. The source of this unhappiness must be from outside. Poverty is the biggest source, but from time to time there might be an unusual blow that drives the family to intense rage. Unhappiness burns the tissues in slow combustion but rage puts your heart on burning coal. You can't think straight and you scream in helplessness.

You can imagine an old family member's death. You can anticipate it and prepare your heart for it. You can reason that the body has let go of this world and wherever the soul has departed, it's going to be content about its role in this world. The old body can't keep up with the spirits of the new generation and contemplates release. That's alright for an old individual. He has worked hard to raise his young and would now prefer to rest.

You can hold back your tears and perform the religious rites for his safe journey abroad. You can tolerate the pain in the chest because there are many others in your family who share that sorrow. You can see a purpose in laying to rest a torn body. But what if this blow happens to a fledgling?

The dog that brought health and happiness into our family was attacked one rainy night by a fox. We heard the commotion and lit the oil-lamp to go out and check. The fox ran away but not before biting the neck of the little one.

I picked him up and brought it inside our house. It lay lifeless. Blood had squirted out of its neck. My mother bandaged him with the end of her cotton saree in order to stop the flow of blood. He lay there for the night. It was drizzling outside, the mosquitoes buzzed about, I used the Sal fan to keep them away from the bleeding puppy. I fell asleep after a while and woke up with a start at dawn. There I saw Deepu fanning the little one, patiently sitting cross-legged by his side. He had not slept at all. When he saw me wake up, he asked if it was time to take Bhola to the doctor. We had no veterinarian in the vicinity. Father said it was not breathing but for Deepu's satisfaction, he offered to take the puppy to the homoeopathic doctor who had once cured my sister's bleeding nose.

Deepu went with him and the doctor convinced him that the dog was dead. On his way back home, he came running and dug his head into mother's lap and cried for a long time. We were getting late for breakfast, but mother did not move him away. I prepared his tiffin but he refused to wear his clothes. He missed school that day.

It was sometime in September. In October, Deepu had a new pastime. We became aware of his need to play with something delicate, younger than him and not intending to hurt his young heart, we collected our small savings to buy four ducklings.

The ducklings were family, just like Bhola. The ducklings were vulnerable just like Bhola. Two of them did not survive even a week. The other two lived for more than a year. The male one was attacked by a stray dog on its way home from the pond. It infuriated Deepu.

We reasoned with him that it was the natural course. One animal preying on another, weaker animal. The fox took the puppy, the dog took the duckling. However easy it might be to treat a member of some other species as family, there was one little shortcoming. That was education. Dogs or ducks or cats and cows, they all live an animal life. They live and die like animals. They take nourishment from our hands but that's about it. The rest of the time we impose our routine, our methods, our whims and fancies, our fears and our tastes on them. Many pets revolt as well. I knew of a neighbour whose female canine friend had turned hysterical by the end of her days and bit his hand. She was taken out for a walk every day, yes, but she was over-protected.

The female duckling grew a little bigger and laid eggs. We ate those eggs. We did not know then that a duck's egg can raise your cholesterol level. We did not know anything called cholesterol. Sometimes we bartered them with poultry eggs because those were more. In any case, that luxury was also not going to last.

With one member gone, we were now five people. My sister continued her studies and I continued my teaching. Deepu had his bouts of rashes on the skin and mother had her bouts of nightmares. We lived on without outside interference for a long time.

The next crisis came in the form of a corn in his right big toe.

After we finally bought him a pair of rubber sandals, he ignored the corn. On the mention of surgery, he said, he felt no pain. He found the sandals comfortable. One of our neighbours saw him limping and enquired about it. We told her that it was the same old corn and she suggested corn-caps. Those were available in medicine shops. My father bought two corn caps and instructed my mother to bandage the cap in place so that Deepu did not have to miss school.

Mother tied the cap with a strip from her old cotton saree and Deepu was satisfied. He was happy to escape the surgery. We hoped that it would work, but a week later we discovered that the corn-cap slipped from its designated place and had no effect on the corn.

The second corn-cap was also wasted in the effort. This time father bought a tape to fix it in place but to no avail. Finally, after another month of excuses, he took Deepu to the hospital again. This time, there was another shocking revelation in store for him. In that hospital, there was no anaesthesia. He must be taken to the hospital yonder, and the cost of the surgery must be borne by him. The doctor was ready to refer him to a surgeon.

Both father and son came home disappointed. They hung their necks and would not explain what was the matter. Now I know, after these many years, that none of them were prepared for the enormity of the task. The corn stayed put for yet another year.

It was sometime after the rains and after Deepu had been promoted to standard four that I discussed the matter of removing the corn with my colleague. She narrated an incident of conducting a minor surgery on her earlobe without anaesthesia. How was it done?

I told my father about it and he agreed to suggest such a thing to the doctor. The doctor took cognizance of Deepu's condition, which was prolonged unnecessarily, and agreed to operate on him without the topical anaesthesia that my father could not afford. He summoned all his attendants and asked them to hold the boy down on the table. Even father was asked to hold his son's head down with all his might, because the boy's body would fight the moment it went under a knife.

The electric cutter was swift and it took no more than half a minute to chop off the corn from his toe. Then the blood was stopped with an iodine pack. The wound was bandaged and Deepu was advised not to go out of doors for ten days. He was prescribed pain killers.

He readily missed school for the first week because of the pain. After ten days, the bandage was removed and we tied a strip of mother's saree around some cotton dabbed in mercurochrome. Although he limped, he insisted on going to school because the wound had healed. The exposed flesh was covered with a thin film of glossy texture and when he walked, this skin felt tender.

Around that time, our sympathetic neighbour gifted him a pair of old rubber slippers that her son had outgrown. This helped. But the foibles of human nature do not show up in times of happiness, but when someone is in pain. The boy went to school eagerly but returned home distraught. Almost all his friends had asked him about his absence and taunted him for the colourful bandage. It was a piece from a flower printed saree and they made fun of it.

The next time, my father bandaged him with a strip from his bush shirt. He carefully cut out a strip from the lower end of the shirt that he hoped to hide under his trousers. Although this fatherly gesture put the taunts at bay, it did not alleviate Deepu's heartache. He was completely taken aback by the contrast between friend and family. He became wary and resentful towards the friends. The charitable nature in him recoiled and he focused more on the books than on the gathering of friends.

Wherever there is great learning, it is accompanied by isolation.

CHAPTER FOUR: EDUCATION

IGNORANCE IS BLISS. It is the happier face of the coin. If you see only the lion emblem, you can't tell how much the coin is worth. To be able to count your wealth, you must lay your coins with the other face up. Then you should also be able to identify the numbers. In the nineteen eighties and nineties, there used to be many more coins in circulation. The government did try to bring them out in various shapes and sizes to make them identifiable from the lion's face up also, but the cautious individual dared not give away a coin before looking at the number embossed on it. That's the result of education.

While distributing wealth is easy for both illiterate and well-read people, the chances are, the latter would think twice before releasing an object from his possession. He would weigh and consider many options, such as how to reuse, recycle and repair it and keep it to himself or how to bargain and seek something useful in its place. The educated may not always act miserly, but they would not even act thoughtlessly. If the gadget has stopped working, he would take it to a repair shop first and then consider if it were worth repairing or if it were feasible to just buy a new one.

Education has that flip side called ignorance. Even the literate people who do not know a particular thing, let's say, about the manufacturing process of paper towels, would use it indiscriminately, thinking foolishly that they were saving water. The same people, if they are made aware of the industrial process, whereby excessive water is wasted in manufacturing paper towels, would switch to using a mugful of water instead.

Ignorance is not as nasty as poverty. Poverty makes an individual ignorant only to some extent. Otherwise, the know-how of almost everything is quite free. It's for the individual to seek knowledge. Ignorance can be found among the rich, the unhealthy, the poor, the healthy, the young, the new, the old and the ancient. Ma Saraswati is not as fickle as Ma Lakshmi.

*

In our family, Ma Saraswati was adored with full faith. Even if we didn't have enough money to pay the fee for college education, we tried to imbue in us a habit of asking for the details of a matter before switching it off our minds.

The monthly ration provided by the government lasted for two weeks. For the rest of the month, my income was used.

As a child I had studied only in the school. If I was required to read and write after school, on those days I preferred to sit on our porch and read in the daylight. My sisters sat beside me likewise. Mosquitoes made a meal of us. We would take one of mother's sarees and wrap it around our backs. It made the mosquitoes attack our feet. The reason was, we could not afford to light a lamp inside the house. After sunset, the only thing we lit was the stove. The kerosene was too little for everything else.

Even after taking all the precautions, sometimes we ran out of kerosene by the third week of the month. This was more in winters when the milk took longer time to boil and food brought home from others was reheated. We ventured to get half-a-litre kerosene from the neighbours who had sprouted around our house. Since no one had any electricity, they were also stingy about the oil. We had to strike a little bargain, deliver some work that required walking a long distance usually, to earn that oil, which was still considered charity. But we held our pride and accepted the bargain.

There were other compromises in our education. We did not get to read a book more than once. It would be a borrowed book and we were given a deadline for returning it. We didn't even write down everything in a notebook. We were very economical about space in the notebook, the single one that served for every subject and that infuriated some of the teachers. We accepted their resentments with stoicism. Working in a government school is not easy. Most of the teachers lost their temper, in the heat and the squalor and the frequent absenteeism, and children bringing in untidy homework. All of them knew our background, we had that written down in the forms. They knew we were struggling, so they tried to keep their temper in check. It was not easy at all.

Our endurance was not an effort. We were simply designed to endure misery. We grew up knowing that there was a great ordeal in front of us, the wading through a life full of miseries. We grew up with attitude. We looked straight into the eyes of the teachers with the expression: we have done our best under the circumstances, don't take objection to it.

Of course, there were many better-off pupils. The teachers turned their attention to them. Sometimes a ragged girl would puke and the attention of the whole class would be diverted to her. The teacher might utter a curse under his breath but instinctively dragged her by the arm to the tap and washed her face, washed her frock too, which was left to dry outside while she sat topless. She was still a child and no one bothered about her looks. It was too hot and no one feared a fever. But that was all. Nobody thought of giving her food to alleviate her stomach pain.

That was how we grew up. Survival of the fittest, indeed, has been the norm. We tried hard to skirt round the difficulties and survive. Had we been dejected and thrown to the ground the only slate we had, it would have been the herald of our ruin.

On top of that our parents brought in Deepu. The ordeal was the same for him. But he took it differently.

*

Deepu was also fascinated by Ma Saraswati. He found broken toys in the streets. He examined a few of them and brought home a broken car one day. The next day he found another one, somewhere else, but its wheel fitted the first one. He found broken dolls, broken umbrellas, torn nets, torn kites, shoes, and slippers. He kept them in the ante-room that he had built for Bhola.

With the ribs of the umbrellas, he made a frame that worked as a door to the little room. He folded the nylon of the umbrellas around the frame and that formed the door. With the rest of the nylon, he replaced the frock of the doll. He found another doll and replaced the broken legs of the first one. He found working batteries in one of the cars and replaced it with the one whose wheels were intact. He worked out a front shield of the roofless car with the help of broken eyeglasses. And then we all enjoyed the rattle of the doll sitting in the car and taking a joy ride.

In those days, he was still going to primary school. The corn on his foot was cut off and the wound had healed. He had regained his enthusiasm. He also fared well in the class and got noticed by the English teacher for his beautiful handwriting. He still has beautiful handwriting. In those days, children wrote in cursive. So when Deepu exhibited beautiful cursive handwriting, with hardly any breaks in the words, the teacher praised him. Soon after that, he had made his own unique doll-car. So, he felt like showing that off.

He displayed his new triumph to his fellows and that was the ruin of it. Days later, he managed to piece together all its parts again. He used a broken rib of an umbrella as a screw-driver and fixed the loosened parts. He spent all day doing the repairs. Once done, he carefully placed the doll and car combo atop the wooden shelf that was built along the upper ledge of the window and it was quite clear from his bearing that no one should touch it.

Education is always sought by youngsters who are not expecting to live a vegetable life. Education begins at home, when a mother explains how an earthen pot is made. Then the next stage is to experiment with one's own hands. Education is a result of curiosity. If a mother does not explain something, a child ventures out into the wider world seeking that explanation. Education does not come naturally to those who labour hard and fall asleep like a log. For education to be fruitful, the child must eat well, sleep well and get enough waking hours to think hard. In that sense, education is a luxury. It comes to those who are not occupied in other tiring activities. It comes to those whose brains are not clogged with immediate worries. When Naren went to Sri Ramakrishna, asking for wealth, his immediate worry, the guru directed him to ask for it aloud in front of Ma Kali. It was at that time, not money, but knowledge that he sought. Because he knew the close-knit circle of fortune-health-education very well. He did not want to get one without the other. He did have a home, though the zamindari system was waning. He did have school education but he wanted to know the circle better. He brought home the desirable fortune much later, after his poor mother had departed from the earth, but he brought that fortune and health to his motherland as a reformer. The complete circle was not only known to him but he also made it achievable for himself as well as his country. We still seek knowledge in the words of the gurus from the Ramakrishna Mission.

To be a reformer, therefore, education is of paramount importance. It wasn't a small matter that a toy car was repaired by Deepu and his curiosity was quenched. When he reached high school, he brought home yet another curio. This time it was a broken radio.

For any home where there was ample income, a radio was a must. The moment it broke down, it was replaced by another. Very few people train as mechanics and therefore, very few people really understand the entrails of the plastic box that got broken by a fall. Once the outside beauty was ruptured, the radio was hurled out of the window.

Deepu brought one such thing and twanged its wires for many days hoping to find enough money to buy some batteries. It required four batteries and we had none. It wasn't guaranteed that after spending on the batteries the radio would work. Deepu glued the plastic body together with the glue of the bel fruit that Mother Nature offered in the month of May. Then he set it up beside the forlorn doll-car.

We sisters were too restless about it. We wanted to play the radio so we collected discarded batteries from everywhere. Those were thrown away after use. We were not ready to accept that four normal looking batteries would still not work. Until, one day, Deepu bought one new battery from the pan-shop.

We assembled them together, three dead batteries and one new, excited with expectations, we turned the knob on. The radio burst into life. It caught a few strains from some distant land and we tried to match the frequency with a nearby station. After a while we hit a news channel. I wanted to hear some film songs but for the day, we dared not rotate the knob again. The sole battery wore out easily and there were no songs the next day.

Today when I wear the earphones on my way to the school where I work, I feel no thrill at finding a new song on the internet. About three months later, I had bought four batteries for the radio, unable to resist it. Those lasted for a week. We had heard many songs and those beautiful melodies from the nineties are still my favourites.

*

The radio was built when he was thirteen years old. About that time, the skin infection had been cured and there were no more eruptions in the rainy season. He was able to attend school without discontinuities. In standard nine he was particularly attentive in class. One day, in the streets, I was approached by a school teacher from my old times, with a broad smile and a recognition that had no connection with me. He showered praises on me for a while as if I had been his favourite scholar. He recalled my name and address. He complimented me on my tenacity to pursue graduation and finally mentioned Deepu like an afterthought. He said, 'your brother is a marvel.' He thought that I was teaching him. I did not venture to contradict him. Deepu studied on his own. He had answered very nicely in the exams. He had the potential to reach great heights. He should be encouraged to take up physics. All that and a few inanities like 'how is your father' to which he did not expect an exact description, and then, he resumed his walk.

I returned home smiling with pride. That little kid, who marked a downward roll of our fortune, now showing signs of rising high! I must tell that to father. When he arrived home, he heard me out. Deepu was outside, flying a kite. Father called out his name and he obediently came in. He rolled the thread of the kite on the leg of a stool that he had collected from the streets. I saw it and thought of gifting him a spool one day.

Our parents were very happy that day. Deepu also affirmed that his physics teacher had marked him as a brilliant boy and

78

gifted him a spare book. He'd called out his name while distributing the answer-papers that he'd checked and told the whole class that he had performed better than all the others so they should clap for him. But he didn't know if the teacher remembered his elder sisters.

I told him immediately that his younger sister was also very good at studies. She had stood first in standard eleven. He was too small at that time to understand such a thing but our family had celebrated the results with a special dish of suji halwa that day.

This prompted the discussion on going for extra tuition in the evening. He had wanted it ever since he was promoted to ninth standard but was afraid of the expenditure. We assured him that he could go, I could afford it, particularly for physics.

*

Although he took tuition for those two years, after the board exams, he had to stop that. My father lost his job again. This time the family of his employer sold the shop and shifted to the city where his daughter was admitted for university education. The parents were proud of her but they were very protective as she was a girl. My father couldn't find another employer at that age and we advised him to retire.

There was paucity of funds and Deepu was the only sacrificial goat around. Had we been more resourceful, maybe he would have earned an engineering degree from an IIT. But such was his luck that he couldn't even fill the application form. Many of his classmates applied and got through the joint entrance test. They are living in posh localities now and we are still here. Deepu left Physics altogether and took up Botany honours.

I remember particularly the evening when he dissected a live frog in our house. He'd brought home a jar of formalin from the school lab. He caught a frog from near the pond and dipped it in the jar. Placing it on its back, he went about step by step, the way he'd learned it in school. There were many children from the neighbourhood who had accompanied him to the house when he was bringing in the frog.

It was a very exciting evening. All of us gathered around him. He was sure that he knew how to stitch it back skin by skin and then it would hop off like a superstar. That part was a disaster. The boy looked on for two hours, waiting for the frog to stir and regain consciousness. He reassured himself that it was just an overdose of formalin but no, the frog did not move a limb.

Ultimately, when it was dinner time, mother asked him to clear the place. He did that obediently, but quite reluctantly took the frog out into the wilderness. He left it near the pond, sprinkled water on its face and hurried back to clean the room. Afterwards, he could not swallow his food. We waited for him to finish dinner.

Father understood his pain very well. We sisters had a hearty laugh at his overconfidence but father silenced us. He asked us to leave the boy alone. Then he himself shoved the unfinished dinner away from Deepu, gesturing him to get up and wash his hands.

Now that I reflect on it, I too feel sympathetic. The boy had learned dissection anyway. His learning would have not been affected, if he had not tried it on his own at home. It was the poor frog's doomsday. He felt like a murderer.

*

We are always learning how to behave in different situations. Even if it was only a frog, it was a living thing which we did not kill to fill our tummies. The intention to kill was also not there. It was helpless in our hands. So many of us turned it around with our naked fingers, contaminated it with our sweat and salt and then we were laughing about the ill-fated thing. In an ecosystem that sustains us, every little being is valuable. They have a role in keeping balance in the cycle of life. That day, father showed with his stern gesture that we sisters were wrong in laughing at the boy for his sentiments. The situation was so special and so unusual and so memorable that even after decades, I have told it to my own child.

Apart from observing the entrails of a frog, reflecting on how similar the human body might be, and at the same time believing that the job of a medic is simple, was a life lesson. In a single experiment we learned that it is not for nothing that humankind takes pride in being able to make repairs in the body. It is not for nothing that frogs are sacrificed at the altar of education. It is not for nothing that only a few people end up being surgeons. And more than anything else, we must know when to laugh at our failures, and when it is inappropriate to giggle and find faults and ungrateful to criticise, make a scene, and also hurl abuses or even stones at people who try to work it out for us till the last drop of hope for life.

Education is a constant process. It is one thing to go to a school to get instructed about a little activity. Such as the dissection of a frog, there may be numerous combinations of concerns and actions that give results. We need positive results. We need to appreciate how ordinary people with frailties and those around them might flourish. We should appreciate medical science to the point of blasphemy, trusting the hands of a fellow being rather than the words of a preacher. We must avoid going to a priest when there is a health issue, and rush to a medic.

On that day, Deepu learned morality. He must have felt it in his heart already but the act showed that he was not an enlightened creature. His evolution into a sensitive, morally aware creature was completed on that day. He became sober. He started observing first before taking action. He controlled his impulses and weighed the consequences first.

Moral supervision is a challenge for the family and does not quite work out well in the school. That was how I understood it that day. At school he did not learn to recognize what is right and what is wrong. Education includes the nurture of the child and his ethos. In the school where one teacher is in charge of one hundred and fifty little kids, the teacher gets exhausted. The teacher might not remember the names of all the pupils.

By the time the children go to high school, again, that particular sensitivity is not cultivated. That is why they misbehave. That is why they hit, steal pens, tear books, break window panes or hide a football from others. That is why, it still falls within the domain of the family and home and neighbourhood to learn a particular set of ethos. The culture one is brought up in determines the child's future behaviour. Once the individual has outgrown the walls of the house, it is next to impossible to mould a character. The family is responsible for giving shape to the mindset of the individual, right from birth. The adult becomes impervious to such suggestions. Constant reprimand and influential behaviour at home forms a solid character, whether good or bad.

The incident of the frog moulded our character in a specific way. The teacher at school could have never given us that life lesson which my father gave us that day.

*

Education is power. King Vikramaditya was a great judge. One day, four men were brought to his court by the sergeants on a charge of murder. They were identified as a teacher, a sepoy, a shopkeeper, and a cobbler. King Vikramaditya called the cobbler aside and said, 'you are not blameworthy as you had wicked companions who did not restrain you from the misdeed.' He addressed the shopkeeper and asked, 'why did you follow the group when you could have escaped by running away? You are not a soldier.' The wise king then spoke sternly to the sepoy that he was not supposed to unleash his fury on a helpless person when his profession was to protect the people. Finally, raising his pointer on the teacher, he said, 'you are the one to be blamed for the murder. You did not stop to reflect on the deed. You did not stop to instruct the others. You did not rightly use your learning.'

King Vikramaditya ordered ten years' imprisonment for the teacher and only two years for the cobbler. So you see, education is power. The educated person has huge responsibilities. He must reflect on every situation. He must instruct others. He must restrain others with his wise words when they do wrong. And words have a better effect than weapons. Always.

I had settled for Bangla Honours because it was easy to borrow books and complete the course. There was no lab fee and expensive books, no competitors to sabotage your efforts and no need to be very regular in attendance. All I needed was a library card. I persisted in those three years without giving up, although at that time my younger sister was made the sacrificial goat. However, I paid back in kind soon after. Now it was Deepu's education at stake and we encouraged him to take up science, never mind if physics was too expensive. He completed his senior secondary school with good results and took admission in a college in the city, twenty kilometres away from our house. This added travel cost was one big contribution on my part, in bringing up a male child in the family who is expected to take care of the parents after the girls are all married off.

My immediate sister was twenty-three when we found a suitable match for her. Our criteria for suitability included the absence of dowry. In her case, we also made the man wait for one year. We allowed them to meet and go for a film and talk to each other. We noticed a growing affection between them with satisfaction. Within a span of twelve months, it was convenient to gather enough funds for the wedding ceremony.

When Deepu was about to join college, we discussed his choice of subjects. It should be interesting, it should fetch him a lucrative occupation after three years, it should not be demanding on our budget and it should not be too difficult for him to clear.

He chose Botany Honours. He was still associating his being with the living things around him. If he had selected economics or computer applications, I would have thought he was looking forward to making money. But when he said, Botany, I was alarmed. I asked him what he was hoping to do afterwards. He replied, 'I'll do teaching.'

Teaching: there's a direct connection. We are descendants of the teacher class. It is in our blood. But to teach Botany and not the Humanities was a novelty. I was not happy with his choice.

It was too impractical. I wanted him to look forward to a profession that made a difference to the way people till the land or control the changes in the environment or manage a treatment unit. I did not want him to go about teaching that there are four types of microorganisms that infect our body and cause diseases. That's what teaching primary school children means. I was already doing a similar thing after studying Bangla. Why would we invest more funds on his education if he was also planning to teach in a primary school after graduation? I told him as much.

*

My sister was married off in a year's time and now we were four members left in the family. My mother began to worry about my marriage. I wanted to change my place of work because I found no joy in meeting the same old people every year. Even if some children were new, most of the parents were familiar. I was expected to address their other issues also, that I felt had no connection with my qualification. I could make the illiterate literate, teach them to write their names and to read documents where they were required to put their signatures. I could do that. I preferred to move on.

It left only Deepu at home with my parents. I noticed that the boy was uncomfortable in the same room. One day, I said aloud that we should expand the covered area of our house. It was possible to add an L-shaped wall on the left side and a door which opened in the front. In it, Deepu could sit with his things during the day and just come inside the house for meals and to sleep at night.

Deepu was delighted to hear that but our parents looked at each other's face with obvious concern. I told him, he would have to build the room with his own hands.

That's when he enquired about electricity. We explained to him that the tower was a long way off on the other end of the railway track. Our village was not connected due to the neglect of the panchayat.

He was not convinced. He ventured to find out the details of the matter by his own means.

Education is a process of engagement with the five questions, why, when, how and then, when and where. As soon as my parents and I drew blank, he tried to look at other resources and learn. He can draw on a range of things to support his convictions and propel his efforts. One of his efforts, in those days of hardship, was directed in getting the electricity line for the house.

The government provided electricity lines only after a certain number of houses had been legally registered in the area. Our house was one of the first to be built in that abandoned fruit orchard. It was at the juncture of the edge of the village and the edge of the wilderness. Other houses took a long time to make their legitimate presence. At first there were only occupants of small huts which didn't count. One has to buy the land from its rightful owner before erecting a building on it. The authorities didn't even bother to find out who was occupying whose land. The owners didn't even bother to check if their land was encroached upon. They were rich landowners, like my grand uncle, who loved peace of mind over wealth. The stamped transfer of ownership via payment took another twenty years after Deepu was born. Similarly, other families began settling around us by clearing the infertile land behind us, ostensibly having bought it.

Perhaps it was the most joyous day of Deepu's life when the last lamp post was erected close to our house. The electricity metre was installed on the front wall and wiring was supervised by the inspector, though we had to pay for the technician, wires, and switches. Though connections were made in the room, the adjacent room for Deepu and also for the anteroom for the non-existent pet, there were no bulbs and fans. Those things came home gradually. The first light in the house was the first sign of better days, beginning from 2010.

*

Deepu earned by coaching children at their homes in the evening. It met most of the requirements for the three of them. Apart from food and light, there wasn't much to ask for. He continued our habit of travelling to the market on weekends to bring nuts, fruits and incense sticks for the villagers. He walked from the railway station to the market and carried back loads of fruits. These were not just for one family but for a large gathering, on occasions when the family organised a Satya Narayan Puja. He was given a commission for the effort. It was not an easy task for him but because villagers offer prayers to the gods for many reasons, the inflow was a weekly, if not daily requirement. He also brought namkeen to the village if anyone asked for it. This was his additional income.

I wonder if I will grow old to be as religious as my neighbours. Aunts and grandmothers take to fasting once in a week, usually Mondays, to appease Lord Shiva. They have grown up daughters and want grooms for them. Some of them take to fasting even for a grandchild, who happens to be prone to cough and cold. Although in my village, unlike the Adivasi ones, most people followed spiritual practices more out of habit than belief, it did mean a large distribution of kheer, shinni and fruits. A lot of ghee, havan samagri and camphor and bel leaves went into the fire. Afterwards, we had the solace of applying a black tika on our foreheads from the oily residue of the havan.

We cashed on the play of rituals, a thing that by itself didn't appeal to us. Nor was it possible to perform them in our house. Our only prayer was that none should fall ill. It was a habit to utter Ma Durga's name when we left home.

Though it was a regular mode of income, for the teenaged Deepu, it took a toll on his health. His legs ached and he wrapped his shins with a gamchha that worked as a compression bandage. Such hardships were tolerated under the firm belief that education can deliver him from the pain one day.

He was mistaken. He takes the pain as a natural part of his life now. He has trained his body to endure great physical activity even as an educator.

*

On an excursion with his teacher, Deepu went with his peers to a hillock which was exploited for practical lessons in fossilisation. It was believed that plants had been submerged in the sweep of lime in a landslide due to flood. The boys were supposed to search for residues of these plants, gnarled trunks, a skeleton of a leaf, a fibrous fruit with the seed intact, or a rare nut. Most students find branches and roots of Banyan trees because these take centuries to decay and vanish in the soil.

Deepu found a rock that looked like the trunk of a tree. He carved it out of the rock with great patience. He had discovered a species of gum tree, not seen around the area, that did not lose its texture in the sedimentary rock. Layers of soil had created furrows on its sides but he was able to trace out the plant part. His fossil turned out to be unique. It weighed twelve kilos and had to be carried by two boys so as not to break it from the middle. The teacher was impressed by the patience with which the boy dug it out, almost relinquishing the chisel and using his finger nails.

The fossil was put on exhibition in the city and won him a prize. The prize money was a blessing as we were approaching the wedding day. I have not seen the fossil but there is a photograph of the thing on a table and Deepu and his teacher and the principal of the college and other dignitaries standing around it. It is framed and preserved in our house.

*

Pharmacy was an easy choice after Botany. A combination of Botany, Chemistry and Zoology coupled with a diploma in Pharmacy, we expected, would land him a very good job in the city. It never crossed anybody's mind that work in the city might take him away from our parents. We were willing to see him rise in society. We always celebrated his achievements and boasted about him among our neighbours. No one else was studying Pharmacy. It is not an easy subject, with all that technical gibberish. He smiled and repeated all those Latin names with alacrity, while we grimaced. He dictated many off-hand precautions to us when we got wounded, though that was rarely with me. It was our mother who needed first-aid most of the time.

When my father's father was young, he had opted to be a shopkeeper. But for tuberculosis, he might have bestowed it on my father as a large business. Then Deepu would have become its owner. My father reflected on the possibility of renting a booth for opening a shop of medicines. We did not think of research work.

Deepu did not think of a shop either. He met new friends and learned about the latest demands on school teachers. One must be a PGT or a TGT. One must train in a B.Ed. college. He learned more about how it works and how long it takes. He was always thinking of teaching, even while attending Pharmacy classes.

It was a prolongation of education that I resented. I can't speak for my parents in this matter because they were growing senile and did not think hard about the future. Their bodies were giving up. One loose tooth from this mouth one day and another loose tooth from the other, the next day. One pair of spectacles was already there. I feared that my father too would ask to see an ophthalmologist soon. It was such a long way off. A whole day was wasted in seeing a doctor, getting the specs ordered in a shop and then returning home with a headache for all that mother had undergone. She was not at all accustomed to going out by bus to a city.

To think of Deepu dilly-dallying with education for too long was like a headache for me. I was alone in complaining about it. I desisted. I was not taken kindly. My mother thoughtlessly insisted that it was better for me to get married rather than spend too much on Deepu. I wanted to wait till Deepu got employment.

He joined an open university to get a B. Ed. degree. Meanwhile, his diploma in pharmacy fetched him employment in Kolkata. We did not hesitate to rejoice about it but he was unhappy. There were no pharmacy firms in our place, so it was but natural that he should leave home for suitable employment. But he remained glum for the whole day.

When he left, we gave him a new pair of shirt-pants and leather sandals. His bedding consisted of a kantha and a mat. The plan was to spend October in a friend's house until he got his first salary, with which he could buy the rest of the items that he needed. It turned out that the friend who had offered him a room, was not living in that house at all. It was a newly constructed four storey building with much of the woodwork yet to be finished. On the prospect of getting a few rupees, he had offered Deepu residence in that empty house. The windows were bare, only the frame was installed on the wall, and there were no window panes. Deepu hung the kantha at the entrance where the door had not yet been installed. The only solace was that nobody would question him about his presence.

At night, it grew cold. He took off the kantha from the two nails that had fixed it, and wrapped himself with it. He used his gamchha to wrap his cold feet. He lay on the mat and planned to leave the next morning.

At his workplace an elderly gentleman heard him out and offered his basement as refuge. With high hopes Deepu reached there with his meagre baggage. There, he discovered that the place had no windows at all. He regretted the miscommunication. He thought the elderly gentleman took his tale about the bare windows too seriously. However, he also felt grateful because at least there was a fan.

In the winters he did not need the fan. In the next few months, he bought a sweater, socks and a blanket. At the end of summer, he discovered that the basement got waterlogged from the rains. At first he decided to pass the three rainy months by keeping all his belongings hoisted up. He managed well until one day the water in his room rose above the bed.

With all these hardships, he persisted and even changed to another pharmacy company with a higher salary. In another year, he received his B. Ed.

That decided him. He would not toil in the corporate sector. He wanted a teaching job. After joining primary school teaching, in another two years, he enrolled for Masters in Education. Once that degree was acquired, he enrolled for Masters in Social Work.

The seeker in him was forever in quest. If not knowledge, what drew him was the desire to eradicate ignorance. Social work entailed a voluntary reformist urge. He aspired to relieve his fellowmen from the drudgery that ignorance drove them to. He saw in his friends, well-wishers, villagers and pupils, the embodiment of ignorance. He cared for their upliftment. His education was not so much for earning wealth, which was faster in the corporate sector, but for working.

CHAPTER FIVE: TEACHING

ONCE WE STRENGTHEN the circle of fortune-health-education, there are no more dark sides to the spectrum. Teaching is absolute fulfillment. It's a sphere with no shadows. Every little ray that emanates from teaching reflects back multiplied. The satisfaction of teaching is a reward in itself, but that is only the first reflection. For years thereafter, the effect of that ray keeps in circulation and rewards the teacher multiple times.

Teaching is a part of growing. The act of teaching is a direct result of respect for truth, others, and the world. It is common for an individual to actively participate in removing ignorance. But intervention in other people's lives is not an easy task. Coaching in the evenings is more like using a steering wheel to take the right path. It is easy. But if you have to start the engine of learning where there's hardly any fuel, teaching entails a whole gamut of preparation.

There are those ministers who order a new design of the curriculum, including hands-on training or asking to impart a skill to the children of illiterate parents. The conferences on pedagogy create a stir and its ripples reach the remotest corners of the villages. The teacher is then engaged in a tussle with ignorance, more often of the parents than with that of the growing child.

Teaching is a journey we take with people. Teachers come into the arena after much of the journey has been covered in the company of parents. Before learning to speak, the child learns how to fill a pitcher. Before learning to write, the child learns how to count on the fingers. Oral communication is dynamic in the family and towards a teacher, who is first perceived as a stranger, the child is likely to clam up.

Therefore, a teacher's intervention goes beyond the family. It is someone who, having a concern for learning, the need for the establishment of knowledge and right knowledge at that, begins the necessary ordeal.

Living things are active processors of knowledge. The aim of knowledge is to apply it in recognizable situations. If a child is told that beyond ten minutes of walk towards East, there is a pond and that pond has a depth of one arm, the situation is a previously learned knowledge. The child walks for ten minutes, recognizes the pond and can fetch water from it without a companion. The rest of the application of this piece of knowledge comes as a result of processing the same information in a slightly different way. The child might want to stand knee deep in the water. Or he might want to splash water on his scorching face. Or he might want to make an about turn and get back home. All these possibilities would be processed by individual children differently. Even the knowledge that filling the pitcher and the return journey would take just another ten to twelve minutes is an application of the few things that he was initially told.

The growth of knowledge is almost like fermentation. It can also be compared to the making of cream or custard. Or one can say that although true knowledge, or information gathered from others was initially only red and blue, the brain has created purple out of it.

The success of teaching depends on how much the teacher reflects on what is good for all. A good teacher has high hopes for his pupils. He considers people's experiences, feelings, and needs and tests their levels of understanding and capacity. He assesses the stage of a child's development before launching a teaching programme. He is not a preacher from the pulpit. Those are religious teachers who do not feel the compulsion to connect cause and effect, matter and change of form, truth and facts. Those are theological teachings that verge on indoctrination of beliefs at an impressionable stage of development, such that it solidifies irreparably. Motivational mass teaching, lecturing from a dais and inspiring action are speeches without consideration of the follower's capacity.

In that sense, everybody is a teacher. Anyone who has a gift for holding an audience spellbound is journeying with people en masse. Such teachers are not concerned with the distant outcome of creating those swift teaching moments, with focus on one thing at the time. Teaching becomes a blessing only when you can purposefully intervene in the way the individual navigates through the rough paths for years to come.

Various things are bundled up in the act of teaching. The ambience, the rapport, the gadgets, the noise, the yawn and the response to all this compose the act of teaching. Furthermore, if there are shortcomings such as illness, heat, pain and distractions from the outside world, teaching becomes a challenge. For gaining the pupil's attention, many other things may need to be addressed. The utmost challenge, therefore, is in creating an environment.

Creating an environment where the pupils can develop as interested learners is not a single teacher's task. It requires governmental efforts. It requires cooperation of the village elders. It requires channeling of resources such as electricity towards education. If there is hydel power, the tendency of the district administration is to switch off the current towards the villages and use it for irrigation in the first few hours of the morning. If there are industries around, the government channels electricity to power the factories. If there is thermal power supply, the cost is too high and frequent power cuts ensure a uniform share of electricity in different villages.

Electricity is vital for the running of schools and colleges. But often, the teachers and pupils would be sweating due to power cuts. Laboratory work may be abandoned for the day because of power cuts. Wealthy schools have air conditioning now. But due to power cuts they have to maintain inverters and these provide for only lights. These are all inevitable distractions from lectures.

If someone like Deepu has still completed his education, the credit is all his. The family can support financially, but the focus and dedication is all his. The children who do fairly well in government schools are in fact brighter than those in private schools. It is just a difference in the environment that channelises their energies differently. If the teachers of a government school are too tired, it is practically because of exhaustion and not a case of shirking work.

*

Fortune can be envious of teaching. Not necessarily does teaching lap up wealth. It is more common to see a teacher happy with one's work than rolling in luxury. Health is probably an ally. Good health is more productive. Family might act as a load to drag but more often, teaching is in the blood and the family is equally happy with your work.

Education may not always pay back. It's a pity. I have often come across educated people ungrateful towards the society and their teachers. Many hard-working people live in a vacuum named ego. They think that their achievements were the products of their solo effort. At the most they might acknowledge the support of their parents, one parent in particular. It's a real pity. We can ignore them if they can live on their own, but more often than not, they actually force their influence into the lives of those whom they owe the greatest gratitude.

Nevertheless, a boy like Deepu who had no shoes, no bags, no lamps and no fans to assist his learning, saw his reflection in many others. It was divine provision that he was recruited in the free primary school through an interview which studied the humanitarian qualities of the man. The curriculum consisted of only the alphabet and basic arithmetic. Primary reading, writing and arithmetic, the three Rs that uphold all human knowledge, from the leather merchant to the aircraft designer, is not a very tough job. All the little ones learned it quickly. The challenge was elsewhere.

Teaching has been almost an aside for Deepu. What attracted his attention was the customs of the people. He found them fearful and orthodox. It is difficult for me to tell how such deep-seated fears settled in their minds. There wasn't any bully in the community. There wasn't a sage they obeyed blindly. There wasn't any supernatural explanation for their fears. But eliminating those fears was a humongous task. It was not just

Deepu who could not comprehend and surmount those hurdles in education, it was the whole bunch of teachers, new as well as experienced, who knocked off the ghee in their heads trying to cajole and convince the elders to send the little ones to school.

These were all family clusters: uncles, aunts, grandfathers, cousins, married, unmarried, divorced, maimed, blind, demented, frail, tired, old, and newborn. The senile head of the family did not know how many members he had. The next best, who was yet not senile, had no energy to take cognizance of his responsibilities. It was entirely unlike our family.

How do we balance traditional practices with the good for all? Many experienced teachers had given up. They said, the tribe was hopeless. They had no one to preach them those ancient beliefs but still they imbibed such things from antiquity. The tribe lived and ate and mated and gave birth in the same way as did their ancestors two thousand years ago. These primitive cultures have receded to remote parts of the country and the government is trying to draw them out into the mainstream. That was Deepu's assignment.

How he could balance his individual needs and wishes with the good for all, I can't tell. I just saw it happening. Those long hours of talking, not to the children, but to their wards; those long walks into the crevices of the culture, watching their behaviour, unravelling their thought structure, and then spending waking nights devising a plan to crack into the unsolved mystery. He did it.

What to do when people do not understand the point of learning things? We know the significance of the basic things like grammar, safety, and health requirements. We must guide people to explore their relevance and encourage participation. He did it.

With words you can't go a long way. You can't tell a child, don't miss school tomorrow, and expect her to remember that and obey you. For her, initially, the teacher, and a newly employed teacher in the school, is just a stranger. Turning that stranger into the most trusted figure in the vicinity is the art of a genius. He did it.

He had great clarity about the specific goals of learning a particular thing. In that community the biggest hurdle was distaste for anything new. Even the letters of the alphabet, the everyday words in written form were abhorred. Why they abhorred the very idea of spending time with reading and writing, was the key to their minds. Learning a particular thing always raised the question, what for. The elders in the community were so cocooned in the everyday affairs of bathing, cooking, cleaning and labouring in the nearby brick kilns that they had no understanding of the world outside their periphery. The biggest challenge was in enlightening them about a space, a range of activities, a consciousness beyond their immediate capacity. He did it.

With the job of teaching, fortune alighted in our home for the first time. In addition, as a favour, she brought fame.

*

With great clarity, he communicated about the specific advantages of learning a particular thing. He told people, once a ten-year-old begins to teach the letters and basic arithmetic to the adult in the family, the circumstances of the household changes. The illiterate father, who used to give a thumb impression on a contract with the dealer of his agricultural produce, can now sign his name. In doing so, he sends the signal that no one can cheat him. If an illiterate mother borrows two hundred rupees from a lender once and another hundred from him a week later, she can do the total herself and tell how much she owes him. If a boy of ten learns mathematics correctly, he can tell the size of his house. If a girl learns about hygiene at an appropriate age, she can prevent many diseases. If a little child can sing the alphabet while playing tic-tac-toe, he embodies the joy of learning.

One monsoon day, Deepu noticed an eight-year-old girl missing from the class. He asked the other children where she might be. They had no answer. The next day, she did not come to the school again and so on. At the end of the week, he got restless. He wanted to know what had happened to her.

One of the children told him that she was confined to the end of the village in a closed room where no one was allowed to enter. It alarmed him. Then the other children chimed in that she has been possessed by a troubled spirit. It caused her shivers and fits. She was attended to by her old grandmother who slept outside her door on a rope-cot. No one was allowed to go near her.

The explanation was obsolete. Someone who had seizures and high fever was ill, not possessed. He immediately decided to go and see her. The villagers tried to restrain him saying that the spirit might attack him too.

He knew better than them. He left the villagers behind and entered the hut. There he found the eight-year-old girl battling with death and apparently the cause was malaria.

He picked her up and tied her to his back like baggage and demanded to see the parents. Both the parents were then working in the paddy fields, primarily occupied with weeding. They do understand weeding as essential for the survival of the crops but when it comes to microorganisms, their understanding fails them. Unless they have seen something, they can't tell of its existence. They imagine ghosts because they believe that humans can die in disquiet and there might be an after-life when they pay visits to those people who had harmed them. Being good to others is the supreme morality. If you even think of evil, even before executing your thoughts, the ghost of some ancestor is going to come and torture you. So, the little girl getting possessed was not a surprise for the villagers.

Morality lies in the fear of punishment rather than the need to do good. Deepu understood that here the ideal would be to take the girl straight to a hospital. He dragged the father from his field and took them to the hospital in the city. There, her blood sample was collected and he deposited her back in the hut.

The next day, it proved to be malaria indeed and the doctor prescribed medicines. Deepu collected the blood report, the prescription, and the medicines all by himself and then turned to the care and protection of the little girl. She took three weeks to recover and start attending school again. This school was free.

Free schools too did not always guarantee full attendance. In a village of seventy to eighty houses, about one hundred and fifty children were eligible for school. In two months, it was easy to know each child by name. At least Deepu kept track of all of them. He taught them the importance of knowing their surroundings. After the incident of malaria, he ventured to collect a few microscopes from the college with the slide of plasmodium fitted into them. He made the children peer into the microscopes and described the microbe. Afterwards, he invited the parents also. Some of them peered into the lens and turned away in horror. The organism through a lens looks as vast as the universe. On another day, he also played a video of the Milky Way projected onto the outer wall of a house after dark.

The aim of teaching is not just imparting a string of words. Practical lessons are more important. How to apply one's knowledge, even the least of knowledge, gained in just a week, made a whole lot of difference. He gifted a mosquito net to the little girl and told her parents to keep her inside it. The aim, he explained, was to prevent her from being bitten by mosquitoes. That way, the plasmodium would not find another victim.

The dictation of the ojha to isolate the child was followed but now, with an understanding of a science behind it, in place of superstition. The ojha intuitively knew that the 'spirit' jumped from one body to another, bringing in the same seizures and fever, but did not see a plasmodium. Those who saw the plasmodium knew what germ was infecting them.

Gradually, he shifted his attention to the needs of the children around him. Gaining respect and following them through their routine, he earned more happiness than what money could have given him. His government salary was enough for a living. He bought a bike to go about places. He found time to observe the people and attack their backwardness.

His first posting brought him to understand the nature of human reasoning, without education. As soon as a child reaches puberty, even a boy, one has to be tied to a sexual partner. There was no other way of curbing human desire. He encountered a tribe that did not understand the sublime goals of life. For them, feeding and multiplying like insects was the solitary purpose of life. The tribe grew in size but didn't develop culturally. Many members even died due to starvation. Many infections plagued them but they struggled to hold together their lives as an integrated whole. It even didn't matter if a solitary soul was craving to free herself from that chain.

The government named them backward classes and sent teachers to those free schools to bring them forward, so to say. I saw them myself. I saw how squalid their dwellings were. I told Deepu, he should get out of the place as soon as possible.

He developed a friendly relationship with the children there. Among one-fifty students, there were five teachers. There was no one else to attend to their needs. If a child was sick, she took away the time for teaching. The teachers themselves distributed work and checked their work and collected data and saved them in ledgers. The teachers themselves managed the gate, bell, the toilets and the compound. There were no other servants. It was all a bundle of responsibilities and the teachers received a fixed salary at the end of the month, whether they loved their work or shirked it.

Soon, the children clung to Deepu for most of the time. It became easy for him to teach as he applied a playful method, taking them out to the compound on pleasant days and teaching them songs. For that purpose, Gurudev Rabindranath wrote many easy lessons to learn the Bangla alphabet. Some of the moral lessons that we still imbibe in our children are inscribed in those nursery rhymes by Gurudev. Some rhymes are based on science.

With his arsenal of knowledge, Deepu set out to eradicate ignorance in that community. It seeped into the little minds, gradually, while probably, at home they faced many obstacles. The school was only till standard four and thereafter, the children had to cycle to the higher secondary school on the outskirts of the village, adjacent the town.

Most children were discouraged to follow education that far. They finished standard four at the age of ten and found work as an apprentice in their father's occupation. Many of them accompanied the adults to the brick kilns or to the rivers to collect sand for contractors. The elders were paid and as child labour was banned, payment was denied, though they worked.

It was a karmic debt they were paying off to their parents. The debt of giving them life on earth. Their longevity was reduced. Their health was compromised. Their backs were bent. Their feet were scarred and their faces were scorched. All this they endured as part of daily life, whereas sitting cross-legged on the floor and reciting a rhyme was considered futile activity.

Deepu only ensured that they attended school without fail. This was also his daily instigation. He told them not to allow their parents to take them anywhere else. He learned persuasive ways, including gifts and parcels of food that most children and their mothers were happy about. He learned that sometimes, if the children had no note-books or pens, they hesitated to come to school. It could be because the teacher scolded them. He avoided scolding and presented them with a fresh note-book and pen and made them finish their assignments within the school hours. That way, he spent half of his salary on the children of the whole community. It, in its turn, showered him with confidence. The village elders invited him to feasts. The parents brought up their problems and looked up to him for solutions. The children adored him and within two years, Deepu was famous around the place.

His heart ached to see his parents. He was living in a rented room. He bought a bike. He travelled home by bike on the weekends. It pleased the parents also.

*

It was a cold afternoon when Deepu received a mysterious letter scribbled by somebody on the page of a note-book. He recognized the page as one from the recent lot that he had distributed. In it four words, 'rescue me from home' were written. He scanned the face of the messenger, a first grader to get some clue about the sender. The boy looked blankly back. He scanned the classroom to find the missing pupil. There were several missing. He looked up the attendance register and located the chronic absentee.

He had already guessed that it must be a girl. He saw the name and decided to ask the pupils about all the other absentees. If satisfactory answers could be gathered about all the rest, it was definitely she.

On taking the names, at once there was a clamour of responses. They all had lame excuses. Any teacher would take those explanations as lame. The pitcher of water broke. The dog was unwell. The frock was wet. The father was sneezing. The mother has taken her to the grandparents. The little toddler needed caring. One has gone to the market as a wedding was approaching. One has gone to get the calf vaccinated. One was looking after a special guest.

These were the explanations for being absent. No one said, anybody was getting married. But Deepu was accustomed to seeing married girls of tender age roaming about in the village. The groom was likely to be of the same or at the most from the next village, and the head-covered girls could be seen following him barefoot at a distance of half a metre. What they learned, how they learned and what they gained from that alliance, it was difficult to picture. It was all very distasteful. He spent sleepless nights wondering why humankind devised such institutions that bore so heavily on the tiny shoulders. It was alright to let the children play and work with their guardians to some extent. Teachers always tried to make learning playful, enjoyable and agreeable at all times. Even in the ancient times, in pathshalas, the sing-song learning, the practicals in the open and the scrutiny of scriptures for insight was enjoyable. Even learning a craft, the hands-on training from the father was enjoyable. The coaching of girls to cook round rotis, the lessons in morning ablutions, the prayers and the follow-up with giving alms were all acceptable. But to tie a little girl, barely aware of the function, with a grown-up who inadvertently roughed her up in order to prove his masculinity, seemed monstrous.

With these thoughts uppermost on his mind, he scrutinised the letter. Intuitively, he felt an urge to show it to the Child Rights Commission. In the morning, he went out early and passed by all the seventy houses, trying to locate the girl's house. He made it out with some surety. He dared not ask about her directly. What he was expected to do was also not clear. The only thing he knew is that the girl would leave the house if outsiders helped.

Taking a child out of the parental home is not a solution to the problem. The environment of the home should be changed to suit her. It was not written why, but Deepu guessed that it might be marriage.

So, he went to the office of the Child Rights Commission in the city. There he was advised to consult a non-government organisation first. Instead of wasting time on official procedures, the NGOs chalk out a plan to confront the family. They also confronted the village elders. The neighbours, who were unwilling to divulge the goings on of the house under suspicion, were more forthcoming to the plain-clothes-women activists. The women made themselves ubiquitous and spoke like kindred spirits. Finally it was revealed that the girl was going to be married.

The family stopped her from going to school because she was vociferous in opposing the marriage to her elderly cousin who lived in another village. She had become fond of learning and was looking forward to attending high school. The eleven-year-old had recently reached puberty and seeing that, they prevented her from going to school where both boys and girls studied together. Deepu was rallied with several excuses and fears of the family. He assured them that keeping her head covered would be good enough. He gave a decent explanation by insisting that the girl was brilliant and she can soon start earning by teaching other children. It somehow pacified the parents but the groom's side resented the intervention.

When the girl appeared in school, many scars and bruises were noticeable on her arms and legs. He insisted that she should see a nurse and get some form of relief. She could not devise a means of seeing a nurse or going to a hospital. She assumed that the pain would go away with time. Finally, Deepu gave her an ointment.

Meanwhile, the parents' faced a lot of wrath from the other family members including the groom. One day the girl came weeping and showed a fresh cut on her lips. Deepu was afraid to go to a family of ten people all by himself so he visited the Child Rights Commission again. There, he was again advised to take non-governmental aid. He managed to convince a man that an authoritative voice was required to show that child marriage was illegal.

They concocted a document of sorts and asked Deepu to persuade the father of the girl to sign the 'declaration.' This declaration, he was to say, would be submitted to the local police station and if they ever violated the law, they would be put behind bars.

The parents were adamant. They feared the family, the would-be husband and elders in the community more. They had no understanding of the police and the law of the land. They lived in a microcosm that separated them from the mainland. Backward, they were, in the sense, primitive, in culture and mindset. It was not impossible to find them riches. It was the openness of their minds that was missing. What they needed was the right window. Deepu thought hard how a belief about puberty can be eradicated for good. He struck upon the idea of sanitary napkins. It was common for women to use old rags for periods. We have also used old rags in our adolescence. He thought of distributing sanitary pads in the school.

The idea was good but soon he discovered that during periods the girls did not turn up at all. He thought of gifting one pad to each of the mature girls, telling them their use. Soon, he procured a video of its use and advantage. He took the help of one activist from the NGO and demonstrated its use to both boys and girls, both young and mature. He thought it was better to let the young boys also know the value of girls' using sanitary napkins so that they would not tease or trouble their sisters and later, their wives.

The videos didn't help much. The girls took the pads home and lost them. He noticed that they did not attend school on the monthly periods. The other reason was cramps. Many of the villagers were malnourished and suffered from cramps during periods. It was only the women who have had one child, who did not cry in pain.

A family of ten can't survive on meagre wages from the brick kiln or the tilling of the land or even selling of milk. If they allowed a grown-up boy to go to a distant city as a labourer, they hardly received regular money. When the boy returned, jobless, he offered his savings. Four month's income vanished within one month. Some of the boys returned as ill and the illness was left unattended. Many of them died lying on a rope-cot.

From child marriage to sanitary pads to contraception. One after the other, the links to all round development became clear to him. He knew the answer to their misery, in theory but he was far from finding a practical approach that would not drive a mob to chop him to pieces.

In theory, being a reformer is uplifting. On ground zero, it is playing with an atom bomb.

*

That girl, he had rescued, just as she had wished, went on to study in high school and is pursuing Masters in Geology now. Her choice was determined by the environment. She watched the labour of her villagers and came up with the notion of purifying the environment. It was an apt choice and she was also able to persuade one of her siblings to follow in her path. She encouraged the others in her college to visit her village and all those girls who came with her, enjoyed the picnic, while studying the landscape also.

It is hard to say how many of the inspired girls had the liberty to pursue any reformist work. Most of them got married in their twenties, some were already married in the middle of their studies. Binding sensitive people to the household is one evil of arranged marriage. This system not only endangers the life of the individual, by tying her with an incompatible partner, but also ravages harmony in the bigger world.

There is a huge organism which we call the cosmos. We believe in astrology, but when it comes to the daily stock, superstition prevails. Where astrology could guide you to make a choice after your heart, the astrologer prefers to make money by advising how to curb your instincts. They instill fear in the family members that the girl would bring them disgrace if she continues to be disobedient. Basically, the astrologer saw that she would not be happily married but he never directed the parents to let her follow a path that gratified her soul.

Even the NGO didis were looked down upon. In that closed culture, which the government labelled backward, it was hard to distinguish the meritorious from the trash. It was hard to distinguish family pressure from free will. It was hard to rescue every child.

On top of that, there was the law. Too much interference in the private matters of any family was unlawful. Because the girl had sent him a note, he felt obliged to intervene. For him at that time, it was a spiritual calling. He must attend to a call for help.

He also had the note as testimony that the initiative came from the child herself. In other families where the girl or even if it was a boy drop-out, unless the child fought with the system, allowed a few bruises to show to the public, there would be no uproar to rescue them.

*

The restlessness that seeps in when someone is incapacitated in the face of an impenetrable system, showed up in Deepu also. He returned home on the weekends to complain about lack of enterprise. It was actually due to watching and beginning to understand the irrational practices of the tribe that triggered his ennui.

He didn't risk being beaten up. Rather, on his part, he supplied free books, note-books and pens to the children. He kept sanitary pads in the school and encouraged the girls to come for classes even during their periods, first using a rag and then changing them in the school. There were no helpers in the school but older girls assisted the others. He continued to show many videos and slides that offered a good understanding of hygiene in connection with sex and drug addiction, molestation, and other abuses. Most of these videos are used by reformists who voluntarily work in groups, visiting remote villages from time to time. Many of them appear as visitors and are taken very lightly, like some amusement. Deepu was a constant presence. He reinforced the belief in learning. He repeated what the reformists had said. He was a government servant and therefore, tied to the school. He had a structured curriculum to follow. He had his limitations and advantages, both.

However, after a few years of staying in the rented room, he contracted the flu that broke his back. He took leave and managed to come home and rest. It was a week after the flu had subsided. He decided to seek a transfer.

*

He had high expectations for all students. Commonly, people believe in aptitude. There are intelligence tests that determine aptitude for one field or the other. There are quizzes that classify bright from dull. There are googly questions that determine your level of wit. Mothers note your temperament from early childhood. Neighbours note your talents. Fathers note your dedication to a particular thing. The doctors note your phlegm.

Then you are classified for a particular vocation. You may do well or fail in it in the long run but from early on, there are people around you who encourage you in one direction according to their observations. There may be a host of others who dictate the trend and who don't want you to deviate from the trend, who don't want you to succeed and call you an outcast or some such thing that shrouds you in unhappiness. You persist and you become a somebody anyway, good or bad, but you exert yourself and you stand on your own feet, raise a family that depends on you and then, without your conscious effort, you become a mother, a father, a neighbour or an uncle who is dictating what a child under your wing should do in one's life.

Deepu had high expectations from all the children under his wing. His primary teaching was to bring literacy to the society. There would be no one signing a document with a thumb impression. There should be no one being cheated by a buyer or a money lender or even an employer. There should be savings, in the bank or otherwise, by being able to keep an account of one's expenditure and budget for the next month. In all of this, literacy is the only saviour. It was the common goal of the society and the government and a teacher was their agency.

Deepu performed this duty as per guidelines. Most teachers never fail in this duty. And indeed, it is a small thing to ask for. The government covers up the rest of the shortcomings. In the annual census, the number of drop-outs is not recorded. In the results, students get generous scores. In the records, there is no registration of marriages, divorces, or even births and deaths. These ground level surveys are conducted by these very primary school teachers and most of them resent being sent for such a task, a thing they never envisaged when they were training to be teachers.

The misdirected energy is a bane of nationalism. Had there been a free society, such as four hundred years ago, with hardly any regulations, no administration and no legal restrictions, many unwanted children would have perished and many geniuses would have thrived. In the present scenario, geniuses are crushed by the demand for mediocrity, the demand to grow at an average speed and mediocrity increases with the attempt to bring at par the most dull and incompetent people. Every time there is an attempt to revise the standards, to achieve higher levels, the popular uproars pull the level down to that of the least creature.

Some say, it is better to move forward together than let the spirited one go ahead of others. With this view, the government employs more funds to pull up the backward classes, scholarships, fee waivers, lower qualification cut offs, talent hunts and various other devices, including low EMIs and more salaries, such as to the physically challenged and women, to let people survive the competitive world. In schools, children are not told if they topped the class, erasing competition, where the genius could have been discovered. So, the spirited one is not allowed to trot forward.

It has the most negative effect on the best of the people. Every average person has a laugh at the cost of the fiery person. The enthusiasm to do something special is completely extinguished. In the ashes of one's dreams, the best people roll in the corridors, limp and aching, having lost appetite, lost imagination, lost happiness, shrivel up and shun the society altogether.

This kind of levelling has its dire side effects on society as well. Nothing brilliant is produced. There are no remarkable achievements, nothing to show in terms of progress. The spark that ignites the imagination and fans the required activity to get the extraordinary outcome, is in a human being. That spark must be allowed to live.

When Deepu decided to leave that tribe and concentrate on home, he was depressed about the system itself. He had done many things, of the clerical and labourer standard, learned a lot of the anomalies of the system and felt frustrated. He was not only fleeing the mob of deeply superstitious villagers but also the futility of working in a system that negates truth. He left the world where the system dictated to him to overlook the obvious social evils. No one from the administration cooperated to rout the social evils.

*

Ethics, human growth and development and social life are such bookish ideals that frustrate the innocent human heart. On job training is way different from the ideals that are taught in the training courses. For instance, it is believed that a loan should be repaid by a certain point of time. But practical life dictates that the loan can be ignored, payment postponed and business can be run until bankruptcy allows you to get spared altogether from repaying the loan.

So, while you are living on the loan, you are buying luxuries, visiting distant places, growing a family, attending expensive parties, feasting and wasting food, electricity, burning the backs of your employees and pretending to be wealthy. A teacher finds all this difficult to digest. His life is surrounded by high ideals, ethical behaviour is of paramount importance to him and it kills his spirit if asked to ignore the anomalies of real life.

Those who survive this on job training, make it to prominent administrative positions and run the country, while those who resent it and recall their high ideals learned in books, recede to the mere function of instructing children on things that they have already begun to doubt.

And yes, great books are rarely written by those who have great power. There is a clear demarcation between those who act and those who think. Writers are thinkers and they can't undo their thoughts so they pour it out in words. Books are made up of such writings and so, in theory, we are always learning what the writers think. In utter contrast, those who act, by virtue of their busy hours and by acquiring immunity towards disturbing thoughts, justify their capability for active participation in decision making and the business of news-making, don't write anything at all.

In fact, one of the ideals of a powerful person is, don't put anything in writing.

Deepu shrank from that dichotomy altogether. He consoled himself by focusing on the improvement of his house and the living conditions of his parents. He was happy with the money and happier to see children learn the alphabet and a few other essential things until they graduated to high school which was not his domain. So, all he focused on was an extra book or an extra coaching and then imparting whatever he believed in and moving on. A child came under his wing at the age of six and passed out at the age of ten. He consoled himself with that.

*

For me, teaching has been a great elevator. It has cleansed me of the jealousy I used to feel towards my parents' male offspring. I saw a spark of greatness in their son when he was very small, and gradually I started admiring him as a spiritually exalted individual.

In due time, he was transferred to his hometown. He could now live in his house and take the bike to work. He hired an architect to redesign his house with concrete terrace and flooring, with proper sanitation and ventilation. He engaged a contractor and got his house rebuilt on the same land. Now there are four rooms, proper electricity, and pipelines for water. One can climb up to the terrace too. The menace of cracked tiles was finally over. The fear of thunderstorms was over. The malaise of mosquitoes and bed bugs was over. The parents wear shoes and slippers. They can rest under the fan. They have a refrigerator and television. They don't have to fetch water from a pond. They have a bathroom for bathing and washing. All the good that capricious fortune was keeping away from them, returned. At the age of thirty-four, most of the hardships were eradicated from his home. All repairs done; it was now time to look forward to growth.

If the worship of Ma Saraswati could very well invite Ma Lakshmi to our house, it was Ma Saraswati alone who could preserve the favourable conditions. Proper budgeting and saving, hygiene for prevention of diseases, proper clothing and ventilation for comfort and proper home appliances for the benefit of saving labour I saw for the first time since my birth. Not even my sisters, who are more or less comfortable in their married lives, could boast of such well being which Deepu brought to our parents.

CHAPTER SIX: COMMUNITY

YOUR COMMUNITY DETERMINES your destiny. The community you are born in, that which you work in and that which you are surrounded with, channels the course of your future. You may be born poor, but if the people of your community are richer than you, they feed your taste for good things. If you are born in a privileged class, but your community is made up of many backward people, your inclination would be to either quit and look for better people, or more interestingly, your mind would be guided by reformist ideals.

I think, if you are born privileged and are surrounded by privileged people, your level of achievement squirts upwards, in search of other galaxies, atoms, adventures and risks. You don't feel either indebted to give back to your community, nor fear the loss of that community feeling. You find unusual ways of burning the fuel in you.

But the more remarkable is that individual, who was born in an underprivileged community, himself poor and still has high goals, not to explore galaxies on his own, but to let the people of his community know that such galaxies exist. Knowledge widens horizons. One born in a knowledgeable community, in the city, a cosmopolis, gains higher knowledge by seeking the universally unknown. The facilities in his vicinity help him in that. The human mind does not rest at one point. It moves forward. It seeks infinite knowledge.

And we all know how infinite knowledge is. In one lifetime, the social and communal goals are limited. The pursuit of knowledge is defined by the facilities in the vicinity. An individual works within the limits of one's community, in his childhood, in his youth and old age. Everything is not open to access. Not every part of the complex world is reachable. Thus, humanity functions as one organism. With members performing limited social duties, the organism as a whole is benefitted.

And one fine morning, when you have recognized your social role, you tell yourself, 'I am the chosen one!'

*

Delirium is a common attribute of people under stress. The confusion caused by intoxicants is more enjoyable than the daily routine. People prefer delirium when the real world is full of unhappiness. Therefore, for those who labour hard in an unrelenting job environment, it is of primary importance to keep a form of intoxicant handy at the end of the day.

Local alcohol is cheap. The ethanol content is high in alcohol and for a semi starved man, easily psychedelic. If other types of drugs are available, everyone tries them.

I have heard that the day's fatigue is extinguished by the hallucinatory effect of the intoxicants. Everyone tries them. It causes wobbly walk, slurred speech and beautiful rolling eyes. It makes you childlike, confused and more relaxed. Under its influence, you can feel elated, act irresponsibly, and risk fighting with someone you always hated. You become abnormal, delusory, and less self-conscious in the open. All your nerves are numbed. Your pride is diminished. Your cognition and your judgment get trampled. Everyone tends to forgive you, except your wife.

I believe sorrow is a direct result of knowledge. To know that some beautiful thing exists, say the lotus pond in a park, and that you don't have the money and time to see it, makes you deeply unhappy. How harmless is the desire! And how harmful is the knowledge that caused the desire. By comparison, perhaps, even though you know that there is Mount Everest, it is very likely that you don't wish to climb it.

Most people live under the crushing fatigue of the day's labour. They do not see that labour as their destiny. It seems to them like a tiring journey towards a day of freedom. That freedom is temporarily available under intoxication. It's like seeing heaven before death.

In moments of impaired judgment, you are likely to wander into a woman's arms, a woman who was not meant to be your consort. Or you can confront your wife with the demand for pleasure and she in her turn, tired but avoiding the self-deprecating intoxicant, just refuses you. Or, there is a possibility that your small house is littered with sprawling children and the only thing you expect back home is roti with a piece of onion and total blackout.

So, the intoxicant helps you to find a world outside reality. You experience states of consciousness that your day life restricts. You smile to yourself and lie flat under the stars, in the mud, in the grass, on the gravel or on a rope-cot and dream of galaxies that reality would never take you to.

The nerves are disengaged, but you think you have everything under control. You count six and give away ten to your dealer and happy with the lovable bottles, you clank them close to your chest. Your voice is quaky, but you confidently divulge the intrigues of your pal. Your member is erect but it is beyond satiation. Your feet are wobbly but you think you are heading straight to your home. And clanking still, you wander about, till a generous neighbour guides you home.

As endless as the routine of work in the brick kiln, is your night time call.

*

I have not seen so much unhappiness under one pale blue sky. Ours was a Babu Para, where most people were well off. We had once been zamindars. Our poverty was more in terms of money than consciousness. We avoided intoxicants and through three generations, strove to maintain an outward appearance of good standards.

We also had friends. But like all good friends, there were very few who intervened in our upliftment. Even the teachers in the school forgot us if we were absent or performed poorly. It is natural for people to be busy, too busy in their own affairs. The decorum of the Babu Para had to be maintained, and one of its conditions was to remain aloof.

By contrast, Deepu ended up in a school that was meant for Adivasis. Adivasis have been recognized by the government as economically and culturally backward. When he had applied for a transfer, he did not know which school he would be sent to. The only supplication was the proximity to our village. He came back dismayed after joining there. He was moved to tears. It was worse than the school he left behind. It was a free school as before but located adjacent to the villages near the river. Very few people from the villages attended the school. He surveyed the villages with growing discontent. He was not inclined to avert duty, like many others do when they are confronted with hardships. He had the tenacity of a mule. He began with the counting and keeping track of all the children of the villages.

*

Many children showed up only once a week. Most of them came in groups of four or five. So the group disappeared for a while and then showed up on a Monday. Their interest was not in the alphabet. They had a different language at home. Their script is Ol Chiki and they speak Santali. Bangla is not their mother tongue. They are not comfortable opening up to people who speak Bangla. The children who are aged six to ten have their closed community sentiments which never get translated into Bangla. Therefore, Bengalis who try to teach them, even if it is English or Hindi, get rebuffed. The students clam up when they are questioned about their problems. They do not even tell the teacher if they have a stomach ache or if they have lost their note-book. They do not share their fears and their minds remain closed to outside interference.

For such children, the old formula of teaching the parents first would apply. But to the dismay of most primary school teachers, none of the parents have time for this. They are not available at home. The little ones stayed back to do the housework and Deepu was reminded of his sister, who cooked rice for all. Deepu was also curious to know if any of the tribes had been educated and went to the city. Apparently, a few relatives lived in the cities but they have not paid much attention to the family back in the village. Most learned Santalis knew

Hindi and English and worked in the corporate sector for a monthly salary.

Night school was a great option. He observed men lingering in the alleys, under a spell, plotting dangerous things, hiding in the dark, keeping away from home. He decided to call into the homes in the morning and offer coaching after sunset. He gave the families an unbeatable argument. Since the children had difficulty in concentrating on the lectures by teachers in the school, he could focus their attention, one child each, by painting blackboards on the outer walls of the house.

In his mind, the overall demonstration of reading and learning would affect the habits of the whole family. With the blackboard and chalk just outside the houses, the children would not be loitering about with marbles. They could just as well copy the letters of the alphabet on the board.

It would bring in playfulness in learning. Primary school children had very small syllabi. The method of learning is mainly by memorising. In addition, if songs, yoga and play-acting are introduced, the whole community can be engaged in learning.

He introduced night time coaching by instinct. He was thinking of a way of engaging the men after work. They observed the children and the children observed them, by default and the menace of cannabis was curtailed.

The momentum was great. All the members of the family looked forward to the arrival of the master and cheerfully gathered around him to learn the alphabet. The entire community was illiterate, so a mere teaching of the alphabet took him one whole year.

He gathered admirers. He was not distributing books and note-books to children as he had done before. There he had grateful people acknowledging his free gifts. Here the people acknowledged his ingenious method of teaching.

Your community directs your destiny.

*

In serving your community in your best possible manner and to the earth's end, you may not find heaven, but you find yourself amidst a group of well-wishers. Charitable people gathered around him and brought money, oil, paint, chalk and many other necessities. Journalists approached him for an interview and he openly posed with the children for photographs. The interviews recorded his sentiment behind it all. 'I don't want children to suffer the way I did in my childhood.'

It didn't matter if he was a villager and the open-air school was in a village. People from all walks of life, conscious of their privileges, donated generously, knowing very well that it would bring about common good if one section of the population is uplifted through education.

Nobody in this country wants to see squalor in an adjacent neighbourhood. Everybody feels pity and helpless. We are doing well, affluent or middle-class or celebrities, we are all very busy people. We spend our whole day, and some stay up nights, to fulfil a destined task that would fetch us money. The sole argument behind ignoring the poor next door is our business. It isn't possibly for us to drop our own pots and fill those of others.

Deepu had the special appointment, chalking his destiny for him. The villagers had no fans. He felt pity for the children. It was better for them to sit in the open in the evenings. His choice was supported by many logical arguments worked out in sleepless nights after he had seen the pitiable condition of the villagers.

Deepu continued with his open-learning program and the children grew smarter. Older children assisted him in guiding others. Mothers and grandmothers poured into the streets, finishing their evening chores quickly, to learn a few things along with the children. The day Deepu showed them plasmodium through the microscope, all the grannies were giggling with high intoxication. Yes, this particular intoxicant had no evil side effects.

*

Somewhere it was reported that there lives a teacher in a remote village who is named Master of the Streets by his pupils. It made the headlines. Soon after, it was discovered that in another part of the country, a school principal has organised teaching in the streets using a microphone. He has directed his teachers to deliver lectures through a loudspeaker.

The idea spread fast and many other village teachers adopted the idea of painting the walls with many useful lessons. The children were distributed mats to sit on, slates to write on and rows of bulbs. God's natural breeze was put to use.

Almost half the population of the village lived with a slight fever during the summers. Many of them suffocated in the rainy season and some of them shivered in the winters. Although in most parts of India, winter is not severe, poor people lack adequate blankets. Deepu arranged for blankets with the help of an NGO in the city. There were around fifty families with an average of five members each. Money poured in through donations and blankets were bought. He then dedicated time to teach them the maintenance of these blankets, as they were to be packed inside a trunk for the greater part of the year.

He invited people to open bank accounts. He helped them to approach the booth for LPG cylinders. He encouraged them to learn their signature. In every way possible, he helped with a vision for their future. He was not providing free rice. His aim was long-term. He wanted the villagers to become self-sufficient, give up their bad habits, learn to save money, and see the outside world through the eyes of a teacher.

Cannabis grows wild in the Himalayas. These villages are in the foothills. Many tribes know how to choose the right amount of leaves to get intoxicated. The degree of hallucination varies and because there is no sale or measure for the product, because these are wild plants, not specifically cultivated as a crop, the sentinels of the law against them can't penalise these tribes. Merely being in possession of some amount is not a crime. It is the sale or hoarding for sale that amounts to breaking of the law. An official ban in no way discourages the tribes from consuming any part of cannabis at home.

Merely saying that intoxicants are harmful for your system is not going to teach anybody anything. Nobody in these parts of the world wants to live long. They take it for granted that life is like that and someday they would drop dead. There is no good in restrictions or discipline or higher goals. They have already attained bliss in ignorance. Ambition is not a term for them. Their understanding of happiness is irrational. Having a numb body for the night is more desirable than the knowledge that it caused body ache during the day. If cannabis can give them happiness, they are ready to consume it, even though the aftermath is body ache.

*

The news of someone teaching whole communities grew in volume. Almost fourteen villages were covered under the programme. Many people chipped in. When asked how this started, the most common answer was inspiration from childhood. The pointer was invariably directed at Deepu. Foreigners seized it as news from the underworld, so to say. Indians saw it as a means of nudging the government awake. Many political leaders saw it as an agenda.

There was a photographer who sent one photo to UNESCO's photography competition and it won a prize. The interviewers asked Deepu how he motivated people, if his family was happy with his work, how many pupils have succeeded in their lives, what he was looking for in a life partner.

Deepu had ignored the promptings of his mother to get married. To him, the whole community was children. In our society, one marries to beget children. With children one gets tied to the hearth and home. It organises life. It gives a sense of responsibility and the need to sacrifice whimsical behaviour is infused in this condition. One can't smoke, one can't use obscene words, one can't insult elders, one can't waste food, these, and many more precautions are taken in front of children. The imploring, learning and judging gaze of the toddlers are taken to be that of God. It is a very tricky way of infusing morality in the household because men, if not women too, would simply ignore mothers, fathers, wives, grandfathers and almost everyone surrounding them when they fall under the spell of any vice. But they can't ignore the innocent eyes of their own offspring.

Deepu had no bad habits. We were not after tying him down for moral purposes. We just wanted to give him a companion, possibly one to accompany him in his mission. The old warning which we are accustomed to, that people of both sexes become insane if their sexual urges are not fulfilled, if the natural course of being an organism is not followed, made us prod Deepu to get married. He was already way older than the marriageable age.

So, when a journalist asked him the same question, we all had a hearty laugh at his expense. We all had a right to laugh at him. Don't we freely laugh at film stars who fail to tie the knot with their co-stars, rumoured as lovers? Don't we laugh louder when the marriages of celebrities fail miserably? Don't the media meticulously follow an upcoming star about their affairs?

So we laughed heartily to think of Deepu as a star of sorts. His playfield may be a little remote and unheard of but he did become a newsmaker. His affairs were interesting for the media and surely, if he courted some girl, it would gain attention. It will become a subject of speculation for many parasites who feed their homes by selling news.

Ever since childhood, he has had a serious disposition. Even though he smiled at children, when it came to adults, he was scornful. He knew they were making money. He knew they found masala in his stories. And he was not at all inclined to provide more masala to the journos in the form of marriage. If at all they came to see his community work, it was Operation Blackboard that he showed them. He told them he was trying to raise the curiosity of the children. He told them he was trying to bring to them knowledge of the unimaginable vastness that makes human beings wiser than animals. He told them his motto was to illuminate the minds of the children so that after a few guided steps, they can see for themselves how forms of matter changed with human effort and how the condition of life can be improved over time.

He showed them how he has taught children to celebrate their birthdays with the planting of a tree every year. He procured saplings from the horticulture department for the purpose. He made the children responsible for their care. They planted those saplings alongside the river and around the fields and along pathways. In this tropical country, trees grow easily. The saplings only need protection from being grazed away by animals. He taught them to protect the trees, water them in the dry season and mark them as belongings. These trees grew strong in ten years. So if a six year old planted a sapling, when she is sixteen, the tree would be taller than her. In another ten years, it would provide shade to many people.

Deepu felt that the journalists were not interested in the trees. Tree plantation was a global project and it was not that fascinating anymore. He told the children to think of the trees as their property and not meant as a governmental drive or any act of appeasement of any authority whatsoever. He encouraged woody trees such as Sal and Sesame. When old enough, a tree can be sold for lumber and fetch them some money.

He taught them to save water. In those villages, taps were installed at roadsides where water from the municipality was distributed for two hours in the morning and two hours in the evening. People were expected to stand in a queue and collect the water in their buckets. Many evenings, if it rained or in the winters, the water flowed freely from the taps while there was nobody to collect it. Deepu taught the children to turn off the taps if they saw water flowing unnecessarily. The government gave a tap once. If it was damaged, it was not replaced immediately. This was a great issue with water supply.

Waiving the question of marriage was very easy for him. He did not pursue personal love, family, or wealth. He told his parents not to entertain any proposals for marriage. But say what he may, parents can't retire unless all of their children are settled. And by settled, they mean tied to the hearth.

My parents did not particularly look for a bride for him. He had outgrown them in stature and people noticed his philanthropy and were rather wary. My parents knew, such as I chose my life partner late in life, outside my community, he might also find someone one day. They only prodded him from time to time, more in the vein of, 'have you found a sweetheart'?

But he finally married someone who is equally enthusiastic about community service. She is a teacher. We had a gala ceremony and invited all the villagers whom Deepu taught. They showered their blessings upon him.

He vowed on the day of his wedding that he would spend one lac a year on one orphaned child in the village. Before becoming a parent, he became a foster parent to many children, particularly during the pandemic.

*

Any reformer, through his activities at the grassroots level, attracts the attention of the administrative bodies. The rationale is that though the reformer was doing a wonderful job, it shamed the administration of the country. Political leaders seize the instance to assail the ruling party. They start visiting the area for their interest in garnering votes. They praise the reformer and promise government aid, if they come to power. These disturbances, though annoying for the villagers, make the reformer famous. With fame, the reformer gets opportunities to press on the reforms. He becomes an example of good governance, work in the district, and standards for the administration to follow.

These villages have been visited by the new recruits in the Indian administrative service during their training. The village became a case study for them. They want to bring about a change in the scenario. They do not know how to go about it. Deepu became their guiding light. Deepu's ideas were recorded and a follow up on the matter, a listing of the hardships of the villagers and how to alleviate them, became important.

Otherwise, looking at the aspirants, it is not possible to find a single being that wanted to visit a village. The administrative officers get charge of remote districts, sit in large offices, send his minions to the squalid areas, and try to plan a budget friendly, quick change in the landscape that showed up brightly in their CV. Thereafter, their first supplication is a promotion.

Promotion means leaving the same post. A prolonged, arduous work of reformation, repair and upgrading of a village is not their target. It is not the reason for joining the administrative services in the first place. Even in a casual interview, the first remark is, what power!

Power is an obtuse intoxicant. The hallucinations aroused by power are not perceived as such. There is no coming down from the heights of paranoia that power infuses in an individual. It is not the same as that of cannabis, sleeping off the effect. Nobody, under the spell of power, wakes up in the morning refreshed and willing to till the land or break the stones once again. It is obtuse to the point of eternal bliss.

With such dreams of power, luxury and fame, these aspirants enter the tough job of administration and the first thing they encounter is a struggling village in some remote district, where power cuts last longer than a day, where water supply is irregular, where education is a joke and the whole landscape is disorganised.

These aspirants looked up to Deepu for enlightenment. They practically had no power. It was a dream and after joining service, it was only a hallucination. All of the administration rests on paperwork, documentation of everything they do. One thing amiss and there would be rivals pouncing on you to drag you in the mud. While Deepu had limitless power in his persuasive speech, in his broad smile and his visionary eyes, the officers, ostensibly enthroned with power, had none.

I had once met a lawyer who had worked towards eradication of child labour. He did not join a political party, conscious of the fact that these were traps, rendering you absolutely powerless to do anything on one's own initiative.

It was the prime minister who had asked new recruits in the administration to adopt one orphan. Deepu was not compelled to do such a thing. He was not compelled to serve a village. He had no CV to submit to a higher official for promotion. He was not making money out of all this. He was serving his heart.

*

The happiness that community work brings has a flip side too. Nobody has grown up in a vacuum. The child was a delicate thing when it stepped into the world. He was instructed in the ways of the world gradually, by the efforts of the family. I spent years cleaning his bottom. His mother spent years rocking him in her bosom. His father broke his back working. His sisters, his parents, his grandfather, all of them were contributing factors in his growth, moulding his outlook and supporting his vision. If he was now doing well, if he was now entertaining guests, if he was now taking oaths to support orphans, he has had the strong foundation of his family to thank.

In all this gaiety, success and splendour, though hard earned by him, there has been the constant sacrifice of the parents. They have been left behind at home from dawn till bedtime. Some neglect, something not done, such as bringing home a bag of rice from the haat, leaves a streak of hardship in the household.

Years of work, stress and worry, malnutrition and incomprehension of the causes and effects brought on a deterioration of the body which was scarcely measured. No amount of fortune in the present could restore the broken body of my parents. We sisters have still recovered, carved out a better life for ourselves, but our parents did not get enough time to close the chapter of hardships and open a new chapter of luxury.

My mother has become senile. Deepu noticed it first and confided it to me, worry written all over his face. He took her to the city to see a doctor a few times. After a thorough check-up, the doctor told him it was old age. Nothing could be done to revitalize her. We just have to take care of the remnants of that organism that spent its energy in its youth, unbridled, and now wants rest.

Thus, our return of fortune, though suitable for the next generation, with health and education and happiness, was tinged with pain to see our parents going under. The moral of the story is, matter changes form, it remains in various forms in various times, changes in composition, lives by division of those compositions and re-grows with new vigour. We are also a form of matter, growing from our mother's womb. We are also burning our fuel and will be extinguished in future. We will see our parents go out and then follow suit. The only hope for the future lies in our children. It serves the community. If I can give my child a better life, I will have paid back for the pains my parents took for me. It is called pitri rin, debt owed to our ancestors. We pay back that rin by bringing up our children. That is in fact, the ancient explanation for arranging marriages for our children.

I am happy that all of us are settled now, in the eyes of our parents. We have given them grandchildren to play with and to feel proud of. We have improved their condition, even if they are retired and feel free to go.

CHAPTER SEVEN: WORLD

THE WORLD WATCHES all our activities. We may close our guilty eyes, but we can't close the questioning eyes of the world. The world penetrates the recesses of our conscience and asks how well we have performed. The body does not rest until it can reply to the incessant voice of the conscience that it has fulfilled its role in the world. The world, though large and wide and painfully out of reach for an individual, leaves its imprint on every conscious being, be it a mosquito or a tiger.

The world watches and reciprocates all our activities. Each of us has an echo in the other. We may not know the presence of the other in our daily chores, but when we lie down for rest at night, there are voices, sounds of the unknown questioner, echo of the sounds we made during the day and the heart finds peace only if these sounds are pleasant.

The world has no alternative. We can't escape the world. There is no virtual world; that, the stories make up for entertainment. The real world is the palpable, changeable, malleable clay that we interact with in our waking hours. There is no scope for hallucinations here. There is no flying away and smiling to oneself in the real world. The real world shrieks out if food is missing. The real world slaps you if the roof leaks. The real world shouts you down if you speak a lie.

There is this world, here and now and livable. Beyond the world, the vast emptiness that awaits us, the black hole to which we give importance, that is self-deluding. It is an attempt to escape the glaring, probing, questioning eyes of the world, the omnipresent.

In this world, where all our actions have an impact, use energy, change the form of matter, and excite ions, there are many hardships. There are delays in journeys, loss of positions, adverse results of a speech, faulty systems, and unhealthy habits.

Let us do our tiny bit to make the world a better place.

*

Save tap water. Villages are dotted with ponds. Marine life is not disturbed by the bathing, washing, and defecating humans. Everything they throw into the water comes back to the shore. It might be proper to say that they frame the pond more concretely. Water drips from the bodies and clothes of the villagers when they leave the pond. This water finds its way back through the soil. The water collected from wells is tolerably drinkable. If the guts get accustomed to filter it correctly, not much harm is done, not at least for the first fifty years of a life. This water too goes back through the soil. Villages are dotted with foliage. There are paths made through the foliage that consume human energy: walking, running, cycling, tearing, and sowing, all the ways in which humans can carve a path across nature. Villages are dotted with clearances, huts built with brick and mud, a thatched roof strengthened with bamboo, a door carved out of wood. None of these things remain with humans for long. At last, they go back through the soil.

But tap water? It is a long winding stream coming from the city. It is treated water. It is water sans the pollutants, the germs and the solids that settle in our guts, kill infants, make people ill like slow poisoning. It is a supply of purified, disinfected water. Tap water is not natural.

It must be a huge bother to identify the tap water, which flows as swiftly as the pond's water, as precious. It dries up equally fast, runs back to a water body equally fast, empties off our bowels equally fast. It does not seem much different. The government makes such a lot of fuss about tap water!

The tap is installed at a crossroad. The water flows from it for two hours in the morning and two hours in the evening. You must take all your buckets and pots there and stand in a queue. If you can make it early, you get water. If you are late, you are at the end of the queue and might miss the water altogether. The queue is that long.

The tap water at the crossroads is not paid for. It looks more like a channeling of ordinary water. It is impossible for an average human, who has been confined to a morning to evening routine of labour, to imagine the processes that involve expenditure, technology, and human effort behind its supply.

So, 'save tap water' is only a cruel injunction. It was not explained. It was not necessary either. The supply was limited, do what you may with it. It will run back to a pond anyhow.

*

Beyond the river is a mass of jungle. That jungle was impenetrable for centuries. The British were afraid to cut a path into it and see the mountains. The tropical forests are dense, with a huge variety of flora and fauna. It's the fauna that drove all humans away from there. Only a few clans, who knew how to keep the animals happy, or perhaps very frightened of them, ventured to make the jungle their home.

Beyond the river, there isn't much to profit from. If one can identify the useful trees, shrubs and herbs, the trick is in collecting their seeds, saplings or branches to grow them in your backyard. So, along the river, it is right to plant a few profitable trees and watch them grow. One day, you can call the tree you cared for, your own. No one would deny you that ownership. It is a tree, not a plot of land that the government takes stalk of and sells. The clans that live inside the jungle, beyond the river, in small numbers, got ignored even by the officials. Other than the reserved forests, nothing is maintained by the government.

These clans, called Adivasis, because they have lived there in a primitive manner for centuries, maintain the jungle. These clans really don't ask for much. They are called backward because they haven't attended schools. They are called backward by those people who see watching TV as a sign of progress. They are called backward by suited-booted Westerners who come from dry, cold climates and see them in a loincloth. That loincloth might also have holes for ventilation; the climate here is so hot, so moist and so varied. It rains after two hot days, and it's sunny again, and it becomes windy at night and one can laze on the branch of a tree, get bitten by ants for all the world. Or we have an ointment concocted from the foliage that keeps bugs and snakes away. That's how backward we are.

We have weapons to ward off intruders. Intruders from across the river ferry across on a raft and try sunbathing. Soon they are hungry, and wander into the jungle to kill a bird. They try to camp on the shore, lighting a fire that frightens the animals. We hear the frightened calls of the animals and know that there are intruders. We come out with our spears and frighten them away. If anyone gets hurt, he limps and jumps onto the raft and never turns back. That's how adept we are in the jungle.

But we are called backward for not attending school.

*

In the cities, the sight of trees is a rare treat. Twenty- to thirty-year-old trees are all white. They are eucalyptuses that grow fast and strong. Their branches are frequently cut off. They do not obstruct traffic or tall buildings. I have seen long stretches of eucalyptuses along highways, bordering the cities.

In the cities, most people prefer trees that bear beautiful flowers. The flowers bloom in one season and most of the branches remain naked in other seasons. They celebrate when the flowers bloom and call it the spring festival. But there's no shade during the horrid summers.

There are orchards protected by private owners. Mango is most common. The next best is jamun. I love jamun a lot but these fruits grow only for two weeks in July. The trees are very tall and shady. Mangoes and jamuns are found almost everywhere, even if the city buildings rise up to ninety feet.

I have never understood why mangoes that grow in the cities are small and sour. They grow almost light yellow and fall. You can't pluck them to eat because they aren't ripe if they are still on the tree. So, you get into the habit of peeking out of the window from time to time to pick a mango as soon as it drops to the ground. It is sometimes very sweet also, as all free things are.

You finally end up buying the seasonal fruits from the haat. There'd be many sellers at once. All of them come from farms, each one having one sack of the fruit of the season. If you go to the haat two weeks later, you'll notice that the seller is the same but the fruit has changed. And if you don't go to the haat every week, you'll miss one or two types of fruit for sure. This is very true for the summer and monsoons. In winters, you actually get fruits grown in some cold region of the country or imported from abroad.

You must attend school to be able to afford a fruit from a haat.

*

The complex connection of school with tap water, trees, fruits and houses is ungraspable for the backward people. It is simple to see a mound of steamed rice as a meal, smoked fish as a feast, and wild leaves as intoxicant. It is easy to see a spear as a weapon, a loincloth as luxury, and a mat as possession. The door to the hut is the gateway to heaven.

To drag an individual from the comfort of one's clan and its culture is like killing one's soul. It requires phenomenal effort to convince a tribe, whose language you don't speak, that learning the country's language for paperwork will fetch them anything greater than that heaven where they rest their tired bodies at night. They are simply not introduced to the concept!

The globe doesn't exist for them. Take the blue ball to them and they might take it for a toy. We need four years of a baby's life to turn it into a civilised being, erasing its primitive traits. For whole clans of adults to get to that level of civilization, leaving behind their primitive practices and beliefs, is a huge challenge. No one, by definition a leader, has penetrated that deep into a clan, coming from across the river, to show them the beauty of the globe.

*

Home is where your mother lives. Home is where you can go back to. Home is a place where you can stay and no one dared ask you why you are there. And so, the government has left them where they are for centuries. If anyone wanders out of the jungle, crosses the river, walks the streets of a city, he forgets his home. It is as fast as you enter a virtual world through a machine and forget where you belong. That man never goes back. He either breaks his back with hard labour on a construction site and enjoys a bun at nightfall in the open pavement, or he dies.

Going back to the tribe is impossible. An outcast is cast out and that's the end of his association with the motherland. The tribe, equally, forgets him. So, you need an interpreter from the outside world, actually, to understand them, and for that purpose, there are those pretenders, the participant observers, the anthropologists, who wear the loincloth and eat the same wild fruits and sleep on a mat. And after a year of penance, the inhabitants see no outsider in him anymore and let him into their secrets. He learns their language by observation.

One such interpreter was Deepu's friend. He had had his period of observing and writing about them and now got back to this side of the river. He told Deepu a lot of things about those tribes.

He told Deepu that the Adivasis don't have a school to go to. They have a different language that is not one of the modern Indian languages, and no good will ever come to them if they don't learn any other language. Somehow, the thought of a school is associated with arithmetic, so, it was assumed that they don't know counting either.

It is believed that the number system that the whole world follows today, was devised by similar tribes that lived in these very Gangetic forests of Asia. Those were still the dense tropical jungles, the tribes drinking water from wells and defecating in the ponds. Those were the same type of people who preferred a perforated loincloth to keep themselves cool in the sultry weather, and they were similarly content with sleeping on a mat.

There must be something wrong now.

Anyhow, we understand that it was two or three millennia ago and therefore, not compatible with our level of progress. At least they were not travelling in rockets. So, even if those tribes had invented the numbers, done the miniscule calculations about the universe, they lacked expertise in technology. Unless, as some scriptures would dispute, they were really travelling by air, on an open-air carriage driven by birds.

And yes, those days are gone. Our level of progress is measured by graduating through a school and university and further on after research, mostly driven by massive egos, and then somehow, going back to a tribe to study our ancestors. It all works in circles, unrecognisable at first, but irrational circles, and there is no denying that we shall all, at last, run back into the water through the soil.

*

Deepu was aghast to learn about one such village. It was way beyond his imagination: no roads, no bridges, no benches, no wheels, no cutlery.

He had been busy teaching under the sky, along the streets, between the mud houses and throughout the evenings, using oil lamps, unless one gentle parent offered to hang a bulb outside his wall. He was feeling so compassionate and so engaged with the work. He had been self-congratulating that kind of philanthropy. He had been, on a daily basis, wiping his own past humiliations and hardships. He had been confronting his dull past with the brilliant future of the children he was coaching, outside of the school curriculum and beyond the limits of his duty for which he was paid a monthly salary.

He had already spread his lessons through many pass out students and other generous folk, who, for want of an occupation, or for want of fulfilment in their given occupation, followed suit. He thought he had reached all the hinterlands. He was hoping to eradicate illiteracy by his efforts. He called his mission, a war against ignorance.

So, on hearing about a clan that did not know of a school, Deepu's tentacles were raised. He lost sleep over this. He fetched out the researcher once again and asked him to show the way to it. The researcher escorted him to the edge of the river and explained the complications involved. He proposed a few devices though.

*

On a Sunday, the summer of 2022, having sweated all night, Deepu took a cool shower earlier than usual, offering prayers in his mind. He had a serious mission ahead.

He kicked his bike and set out towards the North-West. There was a highway along the river but his destination was towards its wild side. He rode on the highway until he spotted a shallow bridge, some twenty kilometres upwards along the river. Here the water was furious. The bridge was drenched in splashes. It was a foot bridge and did not seem to have been used much. Certainly, no vehicle had passed over it. Considering its shallowness, he took a chance. He raised the bike on it with a herculean effort and walked it on the bridge. When in the middle, he looked around.

The river threw a strong protest of a wave over the bike. Deepu's leather sandals got drenched. His trousers were dotted with wetness. He looked for any sign of humans. He had been told by the anthropologist that there might be hidden men. So he looked around for any branch of a tree that might be moving. And he scanned every boulder along the river. He looked down, below the bridge to gauge the depth of the water. It was shallow. The foliage was more of the land variety than underwater. Nothing floated on the surface. No plastic wastes, no fabrics, no lost slippers. There was no sign of human habitation. The water was murky. It had rained a few days ago and all over the place, the trees were a bright veridian. He found the breeze of early four o'clock refreshing. The smell was not familiar. It was probably that of animals. He wondered if twenty kilometres away from home, twenty years later, the abode of the monkeys, who used to visit him in his childhood, would be revealed to him. He felt a pang of nostalgia. He was alone. Maybe he loved the company of monkeys, some company, some sign of life.

There was nothing notable. He dragged the bike forward again. There were a few fish near the shore. All of them were black Tangra fish. A smile crept up his face. He understood the fun of camping and fishing here. At the end of the bridge there was a wide gap. He had to raise the bike on the bamboo frame precariously and after jumping over the gap, pull it quickly and let go. The bike fell on the sandy land with a thud. He stood it on its wheels again and examined it for damages.

When he was engaged in studying the bike, he heard a rustle near the trees ten feet away. Beyond that was the forest. His plan was to ride along the river and wait to find an opening in the forest. He was startled by the sound. He looked up in the direction of the trees and reassured himself that because human tribes lived there, it would not be home for predators from the cat family.

It must be a fox at the most, he said to himself and climbed his bike so as to get away. He started it and sped off on the sandy shore, not happy with the poor performance. The sticky sand splattered on both sides, dirtying the wheels but spared his feet. Those low splatters were common in these places. Not much of the paths were paved.

Having travelled for about ten kilometres he became impatient as he saw no sign of humans. He looked longingly at the other side of the river. Even there, he saw no sign of humans. He was expecting at least one enthusiastic villager who might come with a gamchha to catch some fish.

In another two kilometres, he saw a clearing in the jungle. His first impulse was to turn off the engine of the bike. This made the machine stop at once. On the road, a bike would roll for a few paces. Here, on the mud, it came to a standstill. If he kicked it alive again, there would be a roar. He waited there instead, fearful, and excited.

Nobody came along the muddy clearing. His friend had warned him that the bike was not welcome. It looked like a monster. He decided to park the vehicle under a tree. He was prepared for anything. He turned its head towards the bridge. He imagined himself running back from being chased by fierce people and quickly climbing his bike to speed back to the bridge.

But that was the only defence he had. He was wearing his old shirt-pants and sandals. Nothing new, not even a helmet. In the interiors of villages helmets are laughable. He carried nothing in his hands. So, like they show in the films, he was imagining being carried on a stake to be smoked and eaten by tribals.

It's not that he had never met people of that tribe before. But because those others lived on his side of the river, they appeared more civil. The anthropologist had said that the ones across the river were more conventional tribals.

He had made a great mistake. When the anthropologist was around, he did not try to come here. Now, during the summer holidays, suddenly the idea of exploring the place gripped him. The nights were hot and waking up early was easy. Taking a bath and not disturbing mother at all, he had set out, curiosity overruling reason.

He started walking on the path towards the interior of the jungle. He tried to think if he were lost, how many people would be able to guess where he had gone. He looked straight ahead and used his ears to catch the sound of stirrings on the sides. The path was muddy and insects crawled across it. He had to look down at his steps in order to avoid crushing some of the insects.

Although he did not want to look behind him, at one point he felt a strong urge to see how far he had walked. He also wanted to check if he was leaving any footprints on the path. Since the path was straight, not winding or turning, he had no fear of losing his way. But he did not dare to look behind. The old fear, lodged in the bosom, created by fairytales that say, do not look behind you, made him desist the temptation.

The pattern of trees changed gradually. At first there were banyan trees, but now he saw mangoes. Further on, he could spot bananas. He began to look specifically for guavas. He knew that fruit trees were likely near human habitation. He saw a particular species of mango tree everywhere. So, he gave up hope of seeing guavas and focused on the bananas that were visible from a distance.

The first clearly distinguishable sound was the lowing of cattle. He went in that direction. There was a distinct snorting and then a stamping sound. He heard the buzz of flies and was relieved to know that indeed there was a village hidden in the jungle.

*

When he saw the first cow grazing in the open, he expected to see a cowherd nearby. But by then he was tired and sat down on a large stone. The cow looked his way and mooed. Some other cows came closer to him. He smiled to himself, being inspected by mellow cows, where he had feared furious humans.

There was no cowherd around. After studying him for a few minutes, the cows went back to their breakfast.

It occurred to him that if cows are domesticated here, there may not be any wild animals, at least not in the daytime. But there might be dogs. He sat for a while, gathering in the entire sight before him. The place was open, nearly ten cows calmly grazed away, banana trees were planted in rows, a small clearing seemed to lay waste. He surmised that it was a field for crops but this was not the season for plantation.

Beyond the field he could expect to see villagers. He became apprehensive. He was penetrating a self-contained ecosystem. The question, if at all there was need for education here, rattled his conscience. If he walked across the field making a bee line, in another five minutes he would reach a village. But it was open space and people would spot him from yonder and might dislike his approach.

He looked around for a cowherd. There was none. He went closer to one cow and stroked her just to check her temperament. It was friendly. He started walking towards the wasteland. The cow followed him. This was a blessing. Animals took to him very easily. They smelled the innocence, the benevolence in him. He took one step and the cow followed. When he stopped, the cow stopped too. In this way, he crossed the wasteland and spotted small rectangular huts over there. He spotted a few villagers also. Somehow, none of them looked fierce. And

135

certainly, they were exposed to civilised ways, as their clothing suggested.

The anthropologist had been known by his name. So, Deepu raised his arm and called out that name. The man nearest to him, stopped binding the vines and looked up in his direction. He was wearing a loincloth and a bracelet of beads. When Deepu approached him, the man quickly darted into his hut.

Fear of the unknown permeates every heart. All this while, Deepu was afraid of fierce people. He had heard that they attacked campers from behind the trees. So, he was apprehensive. Now, the young man from the village sprang away from him. It emboldened him. He took the name of his friend again and waited. It flashed through his mind that the man went to get a weapon perhaps but having the cow by his side soothed his nerves. He preferred to believe that the man was only shy.

In a moment, the man came out wearing a striped t-shirt on top of his loincloth. That explained the sudden darting inside. He was indeed civil. He came out and faced Deepu squarely, neither afraid, nor hostile. But there was no sign of welcome either. It was like asking in gestures, what's your purpose here?

Deepu took the name again, like the only mantra he knew. He started speaking in short phrases, starting with 'I am Deepu'.

"I have come to see your village. My friend told me you are very intelligent people but keep your distance from Bengalis. I am a teacher. I want to start teaching Bangla to the children here."

How much he understood was not clear at first. Deepu repeated his lines. He had blurted them out like Naren in front of Ma Kali: very specific. He did go there to teach children, believing that in the modern world, it was sacrilege to let a tribe remain uneducated.

The man gestured to him to sit on the mound under the shade of his hut. Deepu obeyed without delay. The man left him and went further up into the village and called out a name. Another man appeared wearing a loincloth. The two men conversed in Santali. The other man went indoors and came out in a similar striped t-shirt. They came to Deepu and the other man spoke to him in Bangla.

"How will you teach our children here? We don't have a school."

"I will teach in the streets. I have been doing that for a while and it's more fun than going to school."

"Who's behind you? Dada?" And here he named a well-known political leader. Deepu understood that this second man went to the city sometimes, if not every day to work. He replied that he was a school teacher and liked to do coaching in the evenings. At that the man got angry. He said they had no money to pay for coaching and it was 'not required here.'

Deepu told him which school he was employed in and how he was teaching on the streets of villages to pay attention to individuals and how even the parents and grandparents were learning the alphabet without any fees.

He invited the man to see the other village for himself.

The sun was growing bright and everyone had started sweating. All the cows were back in their respective sheds. They were probably going to be milked now. Cows love being milked because it relieves them of the weight in their udders. The calf takes its fill and then the rest of the milk is ours. Because we empty the udders routinely, they fill up more abundantly. This is the way of nature. If something is in demand, nature replenishes it quickly. But then, we must also respect nature. The cows felt free. They grazed about to their fill and they went back to their lovely sheds when the sky was too oppressive. They might wander about for long in winters, who knows?

Deepu remained speechless after that. The men too did not move. He decided to turn around and call it a day. His heart was glad that he had made it that far. As a sign of departure, he asked the other man his name and was told, Hembram. This was annoying because everyone was Hembram there. He knew it but did not say anything. He smiled and waved a little goodbye and turned back, trotting a little fast across the wasteland and then entered the jungle.

The bike was parked in the place without harm. He had to cross the bridge again with difficulty. He reached home by noon.

His heart felt lighter and he looked forward to meeting Hembram again.

Ever since he had heard of a remote village across the river, he had been heavy hearted. His ideal of 'fight against ignorance' was not getting fulfilled unless he could reach the end of the globe with his teaching.

The common tendency of truth seekers is to look up to modernised cities, expect various comforts via education and practice word-power over others. In Deepu, the definition of the globe was directly the opposite. To him, places that have progressed technologically weren't the extremes of the world. These were rather not worth exploring. They are already screaming from the top of multistorey buildings, 'look at us'. They are making themselves the centres of all drama, all strife and all sorts of intrigues, complicated social behaviour that made life miserable for nothing. What Deepu sought was a remote place that was not affected by this attitude of self-display. What he found more rewarding was the self-sufficiency of these small villages that did not ask for more and did not miss anything at all. He knew that Adivasis have lived a primitive sort of lifestyle for centuries. They have not craved for anything from the cities. They have even shunned the Hindu social influences. They did not want to learn Bangla either.

So, it was Deepu's concern that such people should be taught to face the world better equipped, so that no one can steal away their property or come and destroy their culture. He was pleased to see the loincloth and very displeased to see the striped t-shirt. He had never seen pictures of Adivasis in western clothes. They wore sarees and silver jewellery and dry beads made from nuts.

Men in India never needed an upper garment. The country is hot and humid for most part of the year. The women did not need blouses. The footwear was either leather or wood. The cloth was either cotton or silk. The Santals knew weaving. They wore the same pattern throughout the village. They were happy with red, white, and green colours.

Deepu started planning their curriculum. It was easy because he was already teaching in a school for years. But those were children who understood Bangla. In the schools for Adivasis also, most children who attended, knew a little of Bangla. He had made inroads in their villages also, to teach in the evenings and increase their knowledge of Bangla. He was teaching Hindi alongside. He taught the English alphabet according to the syllabus, and arithmetic and the sciences. He needed to plan a section of the syllabus for the remote village where schooling was impossible at this point.

*

Hembram met him one morning, a week later, in the haat. It was accidental. Deepu had hoped to see him only by chance and his wish was fulfilled by chance. The cosmos had conspired to grant him his wish to work for the upliftment of the Adivasis. It gave him immense satisfaction. He was not doing it for the government. He was not obliged to do it for anybody whatsoever. He was doing it for his own satisfaction. He knew that nobody would pat his back at the end of all his efforts and he understood if ever he infuriated anybody in that self-contained remote tribal area, he would be thrown out, if his life was spared. He saw the striped t-shirt as a road to civilising that tribe and he also saw the cows as their unbeatable self-sufficiency.

So he met Hembram at the haat and invited him to climb behind him on his bike and go to a nearby village to see the blackboards on the walls of the houses. Hembram was unafraid, so he readily went with him and saw the method of his teaching. He asked who was paying him for the labour. Deepu proudly said that the government salary was enough. The rest of the work he did was for pleasure. Some of the children ran up to him and hugged him with glee. Hembram saw how affectionate he was and then he asked about the resources.

Many things were arranged during the month and they agreed to start in July. Summer is always treated as a break from school because it makes the body languid, the mind numb and the eyes drowsy. Summer is not a season for celebration but one for caution. Staying under shades, drinking enough fluids, and protecting oneself from strain till the rains provide relief, is all people want.

The first things that greeted Deepu in July were heaps of jamun. The villagers offered him jamuns from their trees and he in his turn shared them with his neighbours. In two weeks, the jamuns will be gone. But it is so nutritious, so good for the tummy and so useful for cutting down fat, people do not wish to miss it. We skip lunch to stuff ourselves with only jamun.

*

Soon, he encountered the problem of darkness. When he arrived at the village using a shorter route that Hembram took, it would already be twilight. He had not noticed it before but now, looking at the slopes on one side and the forest on the other, he realised that the place became dark sooner than other places. He knew there was no electricity so he offered to come in the mornings for an hour. Initially, he used his Sundays to paint the walls. He gave the children one demonstration and then handed them the brush. It was not difficult for many ten-year-olds to follow his method.

He gathered four young boys around him. They were used to the work in cultivation of rice, as I said, the wasteland was reserved for, and were swift in learning new skills. They were the first to draw the alphabets. Mathematics was introduced one month later.

Deepu avoided Bangla and launched into teaching English first. Once the walls had been ready, with his own salary, he bought kerosene and encouraged the children to work in the light of oil-lamps.

*

The striped t-shirt was not the only sign of the intrusion of the outside world in their lives. Men such as Hembram frequently visited the haat and brought home a few gadgets, stylish products such as an iron juicer. One day, while savouring a tumbler of juice, Deepu asked how it was made. Instead of answering him directly, the villagers started an uproar. Hembram explained to him that everybody wanted an electric juicer but since this part of the world was not connected with electric lines, they were grumbling. Many amenities that are run by electricity were missing.

For various purposes and on various occasions, some of the villagers have contacted the municipality to provide them electricity. Their houses grew in number, they cleared more areas of the jungle and laid fields, paddy mostly, and increased their cattle. They had sown seasonal vegetables and the land was particularly fertile over there. The vegetables were also sold in the haat.

They were capable of forging iron and silver into beautiful ornaments and this fetched them a lot of money. With that money they further brought colourful threads and wove beautiful sarees and rugs and many stylish pouches and headgear. These were sold in the haat. If only there would be some electricity, they could improve on their techniques and make more money. They could procure delicacies that are not produced in their villages. But they never talked about education as a dream.

*

Deepu met a few government officials unofficially and enquired about the condition. In their opinion, all these settlements were illegal. The lands on which these houses were built were marked off as forests. These were not meant for human habitation. The whole world knew that tribal people existed and lived inside the forests but for lack of paperwork, there was no acknowledgment of their existence, let alone their needs.

Deepu saw the direct connection between literacy, that too in Bangla, that would get these tribes registered in the common census. Births, deaths, marriages, houses, fields, cattle, all of these are supposed to be officially counted. He asked if anyone had a voter ID card. No.

The circle of fortune-health-education was incomplete here. Mosquito bites weren't a small tingle on their skin. They took on enormous proportions, spreading infections, if not malaria, then fungal growth in the exposed flesh due to excessive scratching of the skin with dirty nails. The connection, though crystal clear to him, was not fathomable for them. The concept of electricity, predominant among a handful of men, did not register in the minds of women and children who hardly ventured to the other side of the river. This tribe was exceptionally excluded from the wider world.

*

Nothing deterred him. He set up his school over there, starting with four boys in the morning. The morning light was bright and the boys were used to waking up early. He took only half an hour. He knew, attention span of little children was short. He addressed them loudly, for the whole village to hear. His aim was to arouse curiosity, so he drew the English alphabet in various shapes and sizes and asked the children which one they liked the best and which one they would want to copy. Many people are good at drawing, even if the drawings do not have specific meanings. The letters are, primarily drawings, sans their symbolism. Sometimes, in order to demonstrate creativity, we distort the shape of the letters to a great extent, something for delight and not meant for instruction.

A letter such as B grips the imagination very soon. Children often draw it on the mud with a stick, play hop-scotch around it, draw windows or bouquets on it. It hardly matters if B is used to spell Book or Boy. It would be a long while before they understand Bookish or Boycott. For the present, it is good enough that they find Bubble an interesting word. The letter W is marvellous. It is also a quaint sound, dublew! It attracts the attention of a two-year-old, disregarding its location at the bottom of the Alphabetical table. I was particularly intrigued by the letter Q, which is an O with a tail and we were taught it with the sketch of a cat.

The boys enthusiastically drew those letters. Four letters for four children. He called on, as a challenge, if there was anyone else who could own a fifth letter. There came another boy and so on. Fanning their self-confidence was more fruitful than winning their love for himself.

The world is always sending us communicative signals. We just have to recognize them. It is told in the scriptures that your immediate duty is to respond to the signal at present. It is usually recognizable in the form of a cry or a wave from a fellow being.

He persevered in his teaching, determined to fulfil his vision of a better world. If he could teach the children of this village for one year, the next year, he might ask them to construct a school. The year after, he might bring them round to teach their mothers. It all took time, but he persevered.

*

About six months later, a few photo journalists arrived there to record the drill. It created a sensation in the media. To find a village where nearly sixty children lacked the basic amenity called electricity, for their education, became absolute slander.

Deepu had not envisaged this angle of the affair. He was invited by the newly appointed mayor of the district, for a refined chitchat. Half of the matter communicated was like a threat and half like a hope. He left the mayor's place with the conclusion that he was being asked to stop teaching at night in the streets until electricity connections were made in the village.

He hesitated to discontinue the teaching. He was not obliged to discontinue because now the media had spread the news and he was serving the community in the right manner.

The municipality took cognizance of that forsaken village beyond the river and worked towards bringing electricity there. The matter was speeded up and poles were erected within a month. The transformer was placed at the end of the village. Many people visited the village and created a lot of disturbances. Deepu had to request them with joined hands to not intrude just to quench their curiosity.

Inside the little huts, there was poor ventilation. The government dragged electricity through a delicate network of lines and poles, but the villagers had to install the lights and fans at their own expense. Many people delayed doing that. They did not need electricity. The concept was too new for them. They were accustomed to their old ways of surviving the heat. Electrical appliances were out of the question. They loved their own methods and did not bother to connect to the outside world.

*

He was disinclined to coax them into accepting the light of the bulbs. It is well known that working in the night light is harmful for the eyes. Those people were early risers and went to bed soon after sunset. He did not want to ruin their good habits. He waited for the families to miss something that they liked. Such as the juicer, somebody soon missed ice. In this way, utilities that were welcome without causing damage to the inner sanctity of the community, were introduced.

It was a great day, in February this year, when the first bulb was lit in the village. It was afternoon and the connections were completed. A tungsten bulb was safer to use and the electrician made a broad gesture with his hands, like the ringmaster of a circus, and lo, by a simple click, there was light!

*

Having told you about all the differences Deepu, the hero of this litany, made in the world, I am standing with folded hands for a little supplication.

This litany is not told to brag about a brilliant brother or a hardworking son who brought back our long-lost prestige, in the form of fame and fortune. It's a prayer for all around wellbeing. It's an account of the world's ways, good and bad both. It's a call to arouse the sleeping conscience of people who boast of power but who move not a single finger to lift humanity from the squalor. It's a recital for purification of the soul. It's an invocation to education, the worship of Ma Saraswati.

It is an appeal to all to help illuminate every nook and corner of the world.

ABOUT THE AUTHOR

Dr. Anuradha Bhattacharyya is author of five books of poetry, four novels, two academic books, over 150 poems published in anthologies and journals and 21 short stories. Besides creative writing, she has written scholarly articles on her topics of interest, psychoanalysis and Buddhism. **Chandigarh Administration** has awarded her Commendation Award for her work in the field of Art & Culture on **Republic Day of India**, 2019. Her books have been reviewed by scholars and she has been extensively interviewed. Research scholars from India and abroad have written critical essays on her poetry. As an expert, she has written Introductions to different anthologies of poems and stories published from Paris, England, New Delhi, Chandigarh and West Bengal. She has spoken on poetry at various institutes and acted as judge in students' public speaking and creative writing contests. She was one of the four jury members in the **Lit Digital Awards 2020**, India. She is currently an Associate Professor of English in a government college under UT, Chandigarh, an appointment through the UPSC, India. She has received the **Best Book of the Year Award** from **Chandigarh Sahitya Akademi** for her English novels in the years 2016, 2019 and for her poetry book in 2020.